Scratch

Stan Rogow Productions · Grosset & Dunlap

GROSSET & DUNLAP
Published by the Penguin Group
Penguin Group (USA) Inc., 375 Hudson Street, New York, New York 10014, U.S.A.
Penguin Group (Canada), 90 Eglinton Avenue East, Suite 700, Toronto, Ontario, Canada
M4P 2Y3
(a division of Pearson Penguin Canada Inc.)
Penguin Books Ltd, 80 Strand, London WC2R 0RL, England
Penguin Ireland, 25 St Stephen's Green, Dublin 2, Ireland
(a division of Penguin Books Ltd)
Penguin Group (Australia), 250 Camberwell Road, Camberwell, Victoria 3124, Australia
(a division of Pearson Australia Group Pty Ltd)
Penguin Books India Pvt Ltd, 11 Community Centre, Panchsheel Park, New Delhi - 110 017,
India
Penguin Group (NZ), Cnr Airborne and Rosedale Roads, Albany, Auckland 1310, New
Zealand
(a division of Pearson New Zealand Ltd)
Penguin Books (South Africa) (Pty) Ltd, 24 Sturdee Avenue, Rosebank, Johannesburg 2196,
South Africa

Penguin Books Ltd, Registered Offices:
80 Strand, London WC2R 0RL, England

Published by Grosset & Dunlap, a division of Penguin Young Readers Group, 345 Hudson
Street, New York, New York 10014. GROSSET & DUNLAP is a trademark of Penguin Group
(USA) Inc. Printed in the U.S.A.

Library of Congress Cataloging-in-Publication Data

Sorrells, Walter.
Scratch : a novelization / by Walter Sorrells and Robert T. Sorrells.
p. cm. -- (Flight 29 down ; 5)
"Based on the TV series created by D.J. MacHale and Stan Rogow."
ISBN 0-448-44403-8 (pbk)
I. Sorrells, Robert T., 1932- . II. MacHale, D. J. III. Rogow, Stan. IV. Stan Rogow Productions.
V. Flight 29 down (Television program) VI. Title.
PZ7.S7216Scr 2006
2006022180

10 9 8 7 6 5 4 3 2 1

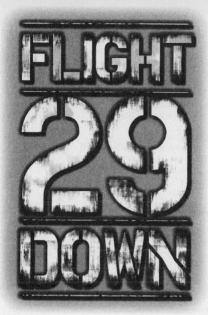

Scratch

A novelization by
Walter Sorrells
and Robert T. Sorrells

Based on the

Mishawaka-Penn-Harris
Public Library
Mishawaka, Indiana

Stan Rogow Productions · Grosset & Dunlap

PROLOGUE

"**O**h. My. God." Taylor spoke first.

The seven kids stood on the edge of the beach and stared.

"It's gone," Daley said.

Just hours ago the plane that had crash-landed them on this deserted island had been lying right there in the middle of the beach. But the storm that had battered the island during the night had swept it away—taking with it a thousand things they needed. Supplies. Equipment. The radio. Shelter.

Gone.

All of it, gone.

The storm that had washed away the plane had also torn up one of their two tents, shredded it, flung it into the trees.

Everyone stood motionless, in shock.

After a moment Melissa felt tears running down her face. "What are we gonna do?" she said, her voice sounding high and weak in her ears.

"We'll start again," Jackson said. "From scratch."

ONE

"**G**ive me a *break*, Daley!" Eric shouted as he pulled himself up out of the airplane seat he had salvaged that morning. "Brainstorming! List making! Organizing committees! Assigning tasks! Telling everybody else what to do!"

"What's your problem, Eric?" Daley said. She'd been trying to raise the issue of building a shelter, and all of a sudden Eric was freaking out.

"I'm fed up with all this teamwork junk, that's my problem!" Eric's cheeks were flushed.

"Eric, grow up! We've lost just about everything. That storm last night wiped us out! We need to get organized and get our priorities straight, or we're going to be stuck sleeping together in the same tiny little tent forever."

Eric and Daley sat on the edge of a broad crescent of beach that extended for half a mile in both directions. In a loose circle around them were the other five kids who—*wow, was it only two weeks ago?*—had crashed here on this uncharted island in the middle of the Pacific Ocean. On one side of the sand was a tangle of green jungle and vegetation. On the other side was the calm ocean.

"I'll let you in on a little secret, Daley," Eric went on, ignoring her remarks. "The West wasn't conquered by people sitting around taking notes at some committee meeting. California wasn't settled by people waiting for somebody else to clear the land for them—"

"Well, they helped each other out, Eric—"

"We've each got to take care of ourselves. That's the only way any of us is going to survive this mess."

His tirade was so unexpected and angry that all the other kids around the fire pit were silenced. When they recovered, they all started babbling at the same time. Nathan cried, "Eric, that's just plain dumb."

"Dumb? What's dumb is you guys sitting around with all your little rules and chores and schedules. Not me. Not anymore. I'm gonna build my own shelter and be comfortable. And alone. With nobody's stink but my own."

With that, Eric stalked away.

For a moment everybody just stared. Then

Melissa hopped up and followed him.

"Jackson," Daley called out. "Stop him. Can't you stop him?"

"Me? Why? It's his call," said Jackson.

"But—"

"I've had it," Jackson said. He, too, got up and walked away.

Daley watched him go, then turned to Nathan.

"God, Nathan, we're falling apart," she said to him.

"Yeah," Nathan said hopelessly. "Like we were ever together. I'm gonna go look around some more," he said, waving his hand vaguely toward the beach, then the jungle. "Maybe I can at least find a better place to pitch our tent."

"But we need a real shelter!" Daley protested.

But Nathan just shrugged and wandered off alone.

Daley looked over at Taylor.

"Don't look at me!" Taylor said. She got up and hurried away.

Daley sat on the sand, looking out at the empty blue ocean. All of a sudden it didn't seem so cheerful. It looked hard and empty, the sun glittering off its surface promising more stifling heat as the day wore on.

Only Daley's little stepbrother, Lex, remained.

"We're in trouble, Lex," Daley said.

"Um, actually, I have an idea," he said. "See, if you—"

She held up her hand. "Sorry, I don't even want to hear it."

Lex looked hurt. He, too, got up and left.

They were in serious trouble. It wasn't just the fact that they didn't have a decent place to sleep. It was everything. They were falling apart. *Everything* was falling apart.

Despite the heat, she shivered.

That morning, Nathan had been scared. Like really, *really* scared. Even the sudden eruption of the storm that had forced their plane to crash-land nearly two weeks earlier was easier to swallow. Whoever said "Knowledge is power" may have been right, he thought, but that storm—the one that forced their plane down onto this dot in the Pacific—paled in comparison to last night's storm. They had been hit by that first storm so suddenly, there hadn't been any time to dwell on their fear, so they'd had no idea of what was in store for them.

But *this . . .*

Standing at the tree line of the beach where the seven of them had been marooned, Nathan could barely take in the devastation. The surf had pounded the shore, gouged out the footing from the sandy bottom, and created fast and dangerous undertows. There was no telling how long it would be before anyone could get out to the sandbar to start fishing again. And right now none of them could safely go into the ocean for a swim or to clean themselves off. The beach itself was littered with palm fronds and fruit ripped from the trees, proof of the devastation possible from these sudden tropical storms.

All of that was bad enough. But the biggest problem was the missing plane. The nose cone, a piece of the wing, a single wheel two-thirds buried in the sand—they were all gone, along with all the food and water they had tried so carefully to save. That wreck had been their lifeline, their hope for survival, their only chance to make their whereabouts known with the radio that had now been blown to—who knew where?

Knowledge like this didn't even begin to bring power, Nathan thought. Only a freezing panic.

He watched several of the others as they crisscrossed the beach almost zombielike—Melissa trying to salvage a tattered rain fly; Lex collecting scattered containers of one sort or another, piling them in front of Daley, who began her inevitable sorting and inventorying; Eric planting a half-destroyed seat from the plane squarely in the sand, then plopping down in it; Taylor, sitting unusually still and quiet, staring out at the ocean. Jackson stood authoritatively, stoic as usual, watching it all. Nathan himself started to do what he could by rebuilding the fire pit, slowly stacking the rocks again as best he could remember.

One by one they all made their way back to the pit.

"You want the good news or the bad news?" Jackson asked when he figured they were all close enough to hear.

"Let's get the bad news first," Nathan answered.

"There's no more packaged camp food. Everything got trashed, including the fruit we'd already collected."

"Well, that's okay," Melissa put in. "That's something we can get more of, at least. We can go collect more fruit."

"Where from?" snapped Eric. "All the fruit trees got stripped in the storm."

"We can go farther inland," Nathan said, trying to stay patient with him. "What else?" he asked Jackson.

"With the plane gone, we don't have a solid place to store things—or a marker that someone in a search plane could spot."

"Should we try looking for it?" Nathan offered. Not that he could see the plane anywhere out in the water.

"Where?" Eric said sarcastically. "Hawaii? It'll be halfway there by now!"

"And the radio's onboard," Lex put in. "So we can't even try to fix it."

Right before the storm swept the plane away the night before, they had heard a voice coming over the radio. But before they'd had a chance to establish contact with whoever was attempting to radio them, lightning struck the antenna and they'd had to run for it.

"So close," Nathan mused aloud, trying to control his voice. "I heard him. I heard him calling us. I tried to respond."

"Do you think he ever heard you?" Melissa asked almost hopefully.

"And what if he did?" Eric put in. "There's no way we can get back in touch. The radio's gone. Along with everything else," he finished lamely. "Like, you might as well look under your pillow for a dollar from the tooth fairy."

Nathan felt a surge of discouragement. Eric was right. Even if the plane had blown just a few hundred yards out into the water—hey, it might as well be a mile. They'd never get it back onto the beach.

"So, what do we do now?" Lex asked softly, breaking a long, tense silence.

"This time we've *got* to have a shelter," Jackson said. "A *real* shelter. Something strong."

The others didn't say anything.

"Shelter," Nathan finally put in. "Now that's a comforting word."

"And what kind of shelter are we talking about here?" Eric sneered.

"I don't know, Eric," Jackson replied, his voice all tired and worn down. "Let's clean up as much as we can now, see what we can find, then meet again this afternoon and get started working on ideas."

I should have seen this coming, Daley told herself as people wandered off from the meeting. *I should have seen this coming. If I'd seen this coming, I could have headed it off.*

Daley didn't know what to do next. She felt that *she* was what was falling apart. *Order,* she thought. *We need some order. Routine keeps things going. Why can't the others understand that? And what's with Eric and his go-it-alone-and-do-it-myself kick? How can I get things back on track? I've got to.*

She sensed someone beside her.

"You want to go look for some fruit, Daley?" It was Lex.

She just stared at him for a second before it occurred to her that he might actually need her right now.

"Sure, Lex," she said, so they left the fire pit, too.

Only Taylor remained. She had been there all

morning, her arms gripped around her knees while the others talked and argued. Had sat there motionless and silent. Not until Daley and Lex left had she even so much as twitched, and then she stirred just slightly, just enough to let go of her knees, bow her head, and raise her hands to cover her face.

She'd been telling herself all this time that this whole thing was a lark, an extended vacation, a chance to make a video that would get her face on TV. Anything but the truth.

The truth was simple. They were stranded.

After a while her mind started flattening out, her thoughts getting smaller and dimmer. Until finally she stopped really thinking at all.

There she sat, her chest heaving with breath after breath, hiding her face from the world she now understood she had to live in. She felt her tears seep through her fingers like the voice fading through the static from the radio: *Two-niner, we could not copy. Repeat. Two-niner . . .*

Then nothing.

TWO

For a minute after everyone had scattered, there was nothing but the sounds of the island—water lapping at the shore, unfamiliar calls of birds from somewhere inland, rustling of the palm fronds.

Eric—Mr. Charity-Begins-at-Home—had been busy getting ready to make his new home. In his head he had more or less moved into his new palace. But because he hadn't exactly figured out what he wanted his palace to look like, he also hadn't put that much thought into a plan for how he would put it together.

Details! he figured. *Mere details!*

He had cleared a space where he wanted to build and was hauling his materials down to it, dropping them into a growing stack near Taylor, who had bundled herself into a sleeping bag and sat staring out at the sea.

"No more lugging water for everybody else," Eric said, apparently to Taylor, but she didn't acknowledge his presence.

"No more picking fruit for people who haven't bothered to pick any for themselves," he went on, arranging his pieces of bamboo—thicker and longer pieces at one end, shorter and skinnier at the other.

"No more listening to Nathan snore. Every man for himself, right?"

Taylor, though, never uttered a word, just kept staring out to sea, wrapped up in herself as surely as she was wrapped into her sleeping bag.

"We'll just see how Her Highness Queen Daley Marin likes doing her own work for a change. That'll be pretty funny, won't it?" He chuckled. "But hey! I'm here to help. Anybody wants something from me, here I am—for a price, of course. The original Free Enterprise man, that's me. It's the American way, baby! And it's how things are gonna work from now on. Right? Huh? Am I right, or am I right?"

Taylor remained mute. It seemed a little weird to him. Taylor pretty much always had something to say. Who knew she could be such a good listener?

"And best of all, there's not gonna be anymore listening to Jackson. Not that he talks that much or anything. But he stands around trying to look all mysterious and everything. And then the next thing you know, everybody's running around trying to do whatever he thinks they should do."

Eric stood and started to slap the sand from his knees, when he saw Jackson standing right behind him.

Oops!

"Oh," Eric managed, feeling around for something to say. "Uh, well . . . well, that's just the way it's gonna be," he said with a shrug. "Survival of the fittest, chief."

Jackson said nothing. He just nodded curtly, then turned and walked away.

Eric blew out a soft breath of relief, glad there hadn't been anything more to the confrontation. Jackson was bigger and stronger than Eric. A lot bigger. It'd probably take about two seconds for him to kick Eric's—well, hey, why worry about it? Eric started back toward the bamboo grove to gather some more materials for his house, leaving Taylor to stare out at the sea.

Daley

Hey, it's Daley here again. Haven't been doing my video diary for a few days. Been a little busy. But I figured it was time to get back to it.

Plus, I guess I needed to vent a little. It's turned so depressing lately. Not just the fact that we haven't gotten rescued and that we've lost the plane and everything . . . it's just that everybody seems like they're freaking out, going off in seven different directions. If there was ever a time we needed to pull together, it's now. But instead, we're falling apart.

Everybody's morale is in the tank. We can't kid ourselves anymore that we're gonna get rescued any minute. I mean, is it possible? Yeah, of course. Some rescue ship might cruise over the horizon in two minutes. I'm not trying to be a Gloomy Gus. But let's face reality: We've gotta assume we're here for a while.

And if we are? We've got to pull together.

But Eric's messing that up. Everything's all about him. If he were just selfish and lazy—like Taylor—that would be bad enough. But he's not satisfied with that. Instead he's gotta insult everybody, make everybody feel like chumps for thinking about anybody beside themselves. Every word he speaks, he's busting us apart.

I'm seriously scared. If this keeps up, pretty soon it's gonna be total chaos.

Nathan and Melissa had wandered down the beach to sort out wreckage and, to their surprise, found a piece of the plane. It wasn't the body, but it was something. Nathan kicked listlessly at the remains of the wing.

"We might be able to use this to build a new shelter," he said. "Or at least make it a part of a wall or something."

"That's a great idea," Melissa said. "You know, I really think that storm's going to bring us together."

"Whoa, Mel. Were we at the same meeting just an hour ago? You know, the one where everybody exploded? Blew their gaskets? Walked out?"

Melissa said, "Well, hey, we're all still in shock, you know? But once reality sets in, we're going to see how much we really need each other."

Nathan's voice grew softer. "You mean that once we see how bad things really are . . . man, we'll be so scared we'll *have* to huddle up."

Nathan stepped closer to the wing and sat down with a groaning sigh. Melissa sidled up to him and tapped him lightly on his head, then sat down next to him.

"Anyway," she went on, her voice taking on a teasing note. "The storm seems to have gotten you and Daley closer. I noticed you were looking for fruit together."

Nathan didn't say anything for a few seconds, but he felt a grin starting to take shape around his lips. He couldn't keep a soft laugh from coming out. It grew a little as he slowly shook his head from side to side.

"Man, she's so great," he said softly, surprised to

hear the words come out of his own mouth. It was totally weird, really. A week ago, he was ready to kill her. Now suddenly he was thinking about her all the time.

Melissa looked at him, waiting for him to go on, but he didn't say anything. He felt embarrassed about the whole thing. Everybody was gonna think he was a total joke if they knew he had a crush on Daley.

"Well," Melissa said, nudging him with a toe. "Go tell her."

"I don't know, Mel. It's funny about Daley and me. We've known each other all our lives, and all our lives we've been enemies."

"You haven't!"

"Well, okay, not *enemies*. But competitors."

"Maybe that's because you've both always wanted the same things? I mean you've got the same values and all?"

"I guess, but we really go at things in different ways. For her, everything's, like, outline form. You know? Roman numeral I-II-III, A-B-C, 1-2-3, little letter a-b-c. You know what I mean? I don't go at life that way. I'm more 'shoot from the hip.'"

"You're overthinking this. Just *tell* her, Nathan! She needs to hear it from you."

Nathan shook his head. He couldn't do it. The whole thing was just too goofy. "No way, Mel. If I tell her how much I really like her and she shoots me down, there's no place to hide. We're in each other's faces 24/7."

He caught Melissa's eye, and she looked away, as if she sensed his embarrassment. "Okay," she said after a minute. "That's all true. But sometimes opposites attract. What if she likes you, too?"

"Yeah, right! Me? Come on, she hates everything I stand for. Besides, I'm too much of a threat to her."

"A threat!"

"You know what I mean. She's gotta be in charge. If she started liking me, it'd make her feel . . . weak. And you know how much she hates that."

Melissa raised one eyebrow. She didn't seem to have much of a comeback for that.

"But even, okay, let's say you're right," he went on. "Let's say she's totally digging me. How can we start any kind of relationship here? There's too much going on. Too much . . . *stuff*!"

"Yeah, I know how you feel. That's what Jackson said, too. But at least he knows how I feel about him. Truth is a good thing," she ended brightly. "It really is. In the long run."

"And if she laughs in my face? Well, stand back 'cause I'd have to start swimming home."

Melissa laughed and stood up. "Guess we better get back to work."

Sometimes it seemed like all they did here was work.

Daley switched off the video camera and tried to figure what to do next. There was so much to do, it almost seemed impossible.

She had pretty much finished taking inventory of their stuff and figured out what had been lost in the storm and what had simply been blown somewhere else—or buried in the sand. She'd found a couple of bags of trail food and some other odds and ends strewn up and down the beach, including some of their tools. But otherwise? Not too much had made it. Still, there was plenty of heavy work to do, so she went back to see if she could shame Taylor into getting up off her duff.

She took the video camera—luckily they'd been holding it in their tent, or it'd be lost, too—and walked down the beach until she reached the fire pit. Taylor was still sitting there looking all miserable. Probably hoping everybody'd feel sympathetic for her so they'd do her work.

Sorry, sweetie pie. Not gonna play that game.

"Taylor!" Daley snapped her fingers in front of Taylor's face. "Earth to Taylor. There's a lot to do. I could really use some help around here."

Taylor continued to sit right as she had been, still staring out at the ocean.

"Um, hel*lo*!" Daley felt the sarcasm creeping into her voice. "In case you missed it, our whole world just got destroyed. I totally forgot to bring my maid and my butler, so there's nobody else around to put it back together except us."

She paused.

"Us, Taylor. That includes you."

Still, there was no response from Taylor. It was a little odd, actually. Usually Taylor had to come back at you with some kind of poor attempt at a smart remark. But she didn't even seem to be aware of Daley's presence.

"Taylor!" she exploded. "This isn't funny!" She heard the rising edge of fear and anger in her own voice, but Taylor stayed exactly where she was, still unmoving.

Disgusted, Daley started to walk away, working hard to control her anger and her own frustration. Then she turned back.

"Fine!" she nearly screamed. "You just go on and hang out in denial while the rest of us at least try to cope. But I'm telling you this, Taylor: There's no salvation out here. There's nobody to ride in on a white stallion to rescue us. There's no glamour photographer to swoop down from a pink cloud and sweep you up in his arms while he presents you with a movie contract. There's no cavalry out here, Taylor. There's no butler, there's no maid, there's no daddy, no nothing. We're all we've got."

With that, Daley stalked off.

Jackson had been heading out of the jungle after looking for fruit. But as he reached the tree line, he heard a raised voice. Daley, as usual, railing at somebody. As he got a little closer, he saw Taylor huddled up in her sleeping bag next to the wet remains of the fire. Daley stood over her, yelling, her face red. Finally, she ran out of steam and stomped away.

After she left, Taylor's back and shoulders began convulsing.

Taylor wasn't faking it. Jackson could tell she was sobbing for real. Real tears.

Lex wandered through the jungle, exploring a new path. It always made him a little nervous, veering off the familiar walkways they'd beaten out. All you had to do was get ten feet off one of the old paths and you could suddenly feel totally lost in the dense jungle. It was easy to get creeped out pretty quickly if you let yourself. But if you thought about it—all these trees were their friends. Every single tree had a thousand uses. You could make boards out of them, you could strip off bark to make rope, you could eat the fruit. And then there was bamboo. Bamboo was actually a grass, not a tree. But it was amazingly useful stuff.

His thoughts went back to his project, this thing he'd been working on for a few days now— one that would help them all, big-time.

If it worked.

But he was afraid of what the storm might have

done to his project, so he felt unusually nervous.

He came out of the trees into a little scrubby clearing.

Then he saw it.

He stopped, took a deep breath, and surveyed his handiwork. The large tarp he had dragged out of the plane the first day when the others were busy worrying about other things lay on the ground right where he had put it. It was held down by rocks along all four edges. He knew the storm could have wiped everything out, so he kneeled at one corner, closed his eyes, and took another deep breath.

Then he opened his eyes and lifted up the corner. He smiled a little and peeled back more and more of the tarp.

"Yes!" he shouted. "Yes! Yes! Yes!" He pumped his arm and fist in the air. His little project was fine.

Carefully, he replaced the tarp so the ground it had covered was again protected. Lex started walking back to the beach, a satisfied smile on his face.

THREE

Near the fire pit Daley was struggling with a rain fly, trying to turn it into a makeshift sun shelter for storing the fruit that people were bringing back from the jungle.

She knew what she wanted it to do, but she didn't have any perfect-size sticks or pegs to make the thing stand by itself, and the sand wasn't the easiest stuff to try to pound or push the make-do bamboo into, so she was having to . . .

"Nathan," she finally said, "if you could find a way to get *that* stick in at the same time I was getting *this* stick in, I think it would go easier."

"Oh, sure," he answered enthusiastically. Daley was a little surprised. Normally he had to chip in with his own idea about how to do everything, and then they had to argue while he tried to prove that his idea was better than hers. It was kind of odd, but he'd been really sweet lately. She couldn't even remember the last time they'd argued. It seemed like they were just . . . in sync. Weird.

They started working, quickly getting into a rhythm. Once it became clear that they'd have the fly set up quickly, Daley opened up the topic she was really concerned with.

"You know what this was?" she asked.

Nathan grunted slightly, but didn't answer.

"It was a wake-up call," she went on.

"Absolutely," Nathan replied. "I was so absolutely waked up by it all!"

"Umm . . . okay. But we need to rely on each other now more than ever."

"Absolutely, Daley. I mean, I was feeling the same thing. Exactly!" His brown eyes were wide, looking straight into hers. "Man, we seem to be thinking on the same track. So it kinda seemed to me that—"

"Nathan, it isn't about *think*ing. It's about *do*ing." She pointed at his end of the rain fly. "Pull your side a little tighter."

"Right," he said, increasing the tension by just the perfect amount. "*Do*ing. Absolutely. All about doing."

Daley gave him some makeshift pegs that Lex had fashioned from a splintered palm tree. She gave him brief instructions on where to put them and how to drive them into the sand. He completed the task without the slightest complaint, without interjecting ten brilliant ideas about how to do it better and faster, or about how his great-great-grandfather, the famous explorer, had written in his book that you were supposed to do it.

When he was done, Nathan said, "So, like, exactly what were you suggesting? Where were you going with this train of thought?" He sounded unusually formal. It almost made her suspicious. If it had been Eric, she would have known he was trying to manipulate her. But that wasn't Nathan's way. Give him credit, you knew where you stood with Nathan. He was a genuine guy.

"We've got to set an example," Daley answered.

"Absolutely," he responded decisively. "We'll lead by example."

"No, Nathan," she said, peering at him over the fly. "It's not our job to *lead*."

"Ah, well, uh, right." He nodded his head furiously. "I mean, *leading* may not be the right word exactly."

Daley hammered in the last peg.

"There," she said. "That's about as good as it's going to get right now, I guess."

"It is?"

Daley simply stared at him for a second.

"The rain fly, Nathan. That's about as good as we can get it right now."

"Oh. Well, yeah," he said, stepping back just a little to give their handiwork an appraising look.

"*Leading*, Nathan, is not *our* job. Jackson is our

leader. If we're going to have a system that works, we've got to stick by what we agreed to. Jackson has to step up and take charge, and what we've got to do is back him up. *That's* our job."

"Right. For the *system* to work. The *system* has to work." Nathan paused, still nodding. His voice sounded tentative. "Right?"

"Exactly," Daley said. "I think you've got it now."

With that, they collected a few things and Daley straightened up around the fire pit a little. Nathan scurried around, helping without complaint.

Jackson stepped from behind the cover of some shrubs and trees where he had paused when he saw Daley and Nathan together. He hadn't meant to be eavesdropping, but he had heard the end of their conversation pretty clearly.

And he wasn't at all happy about it.

This leadership junk was for the birds.

Eric had cleared his area just enough to mark off the perimeter of his new house.

Not wasting a bunch of time clearing extra stuff. Just the exact right amount. No more, no less.

He had gathered what looked to him like

enough bamboo sticks to make a good frame and tied them together at the top into a teepee shape. He had done some thinking and decided that a teepee was the absolute easiest structure on the planet to build. Why make something complicated when you could make something easy? He was now covering the teepee with palm fronds he'd gathered up from the forest floor. Layer enough of them and the water would run right off the sides when it rained.

Beautiful! he thought as he worked. *Am I a genius or what?*

While Eric was working, Lex came wandering out of the woods and stood there for a while staring at Eric. Eric had come up with a simple method for layering the palm fronds, mostly just laying them on the bamboo, then tucking them in here and there if they started to slide to the ground. Lex watched intently without speaking.

Having the kid stare at him got real irritating, real fast. Eric didn't like anybody watching him work.

"You're welcome to help!" Eric smiled. Butter the kid up a little, maybe Eric could lie back, let Lex do all the work. "You're the junior engineer— feel free to jump in, show me how it's done."

"Hm," Lex said.

"Nice design though, huh? Max results, minimum effort. While all the rest of you guys are crammed in that crummy, tiny, stinking tent, I'm going to be living here in my own place."

Lex said nothing. He made no move to help. It didn't bother Eric. In fact, he was feeling a little cocky now—the whole thing was coming together like clockwork. It was like his mom always said: "Eric's brilliant. He just doesn't apply himself."

Well, she was right. But you had to pick your moments, know when to apply yourself, and when not to. This happened to be one of those rare moments.

"See, if I've got to smell anybody's stinky feet, at least they're going to be my own."

Lex looked at the structure skeptically, blinking through his glasses.

"This—TA-DA!—is the wave of my future on this stupid island," Eric said. "Behold, little one, and take note of my massive architectural brilliance."

Lex scooted closer to the thing and took hold of one of the bamboo rods Eric had planted at the base of his more or less conical building. He shook it vigorously. The whole thing trembled, and a number of the fronds slid to the sand.

"Hey," Eric yelled at Lex. "Cut that out. You're messing it up."

"How long do you really think that's going to stand up, Eric?"

Eric stared at his teepee, then at Lex. What was the kid's problem? He was getting Daley Disease, turning into another fountain of negativity.

"Well, obviously, it's not totally finished yet," Eric said loftily. "It'll stand up better than that smelly tent you'll be living in. If you can even call that living."

"And when it rains? Or the wind blows?"

"Beat it," Eric sneered, making shooing motions with both hands. "It's not even done yet, you little jerk."

"You need some more support, Eric. You need some of those smaller trees over there. You've got to build a base, not just stick some bamboo poles in the sand. And the way you've secured the poles at the top? Frankly, that seems insufficiently—"

"Frankly"—Eric put all the sarcasm he could in his voice—"how about you *go away*. Shoo, Lex! I don't need your help, little boy. Save it for those dummies who want to rule the world over there."

Lex stood up and stared at Eric for about three seconds before he turned, shrugged his shoulders, then headed back toward the tree line.

Eric watched him leave and shook his head slowly. "Jeez," he spit out. Then he looked at his morning's work. He reached out to touch the skin of his home, patting it just a little. It seemed sturdy enough. Then, feeling encouraged, he gave the thing a shake. It wobbled a little. And yeah, maybe a couple of palm fronds fell out. But it was fine. No problemo. He shook it again.

See? he thought. *Solid as a rock.*

Then a gust of wind kicked up and the structure shimmied slightly, all the palm fronds jiggling in the breeze. And then, with a slow, stately clatter of bamboo and palm fronds, the entire thing slid over sideways and fell in a heap.

Eric stared at it bleakly, feeling a stab of discouragement. It looked like a pile of garbage. He peered around quickly to see if anybody was looking. Suddenly he was aware of how blistered his hands were from cutting bamboo; how his arms were sore; how his skin was covered with papery bits of bamboo and palm fronds.

He wanted to sink down in a heap.

But then they'd all laugh at him. He kicked savagely at one of the fallen poles. Then he dragged it out and prepared to start all over again.

He felt a bitter little smile forming on his lips. *This time it's gonna be perfect! They'll see. They'll all see!*

Melissa saw Jackson down near the shore, sitting alone on the wing of the now-absent plane. She meandered toward him, not wanting to disturb him, but also wanting to be with him, no matter what his mood was. She put on her happy face, the one she preferred the world to see.

"Hey," she called cheerfully. "Planning our next move, O Great Leader?"

Jackson looked up slowly, stretching a little to unkink his legs. He didn't seem all that enthusiastic to see her.

"Yeah. I guess. Something like that."

"Well, I'm not worried," Melissa said. "Eric's just being Eric, and Taylor's not much help anyway. But at least Nathan and Daley aren't fighting anymore. And you *know* I'm on your side. Right? So all you have to do is figure out a way to get us all on the same page—"

Jackson cut her off with a little snort.

"Yeah. Right. I'll be thinking about that, too, Melissa," he said quietly.

He got to his feet, and without another word walked away slowly, his head down, hands jammed into his pockets, scuffing his feet at the sand.

Melissa's face fell. She watched him walk away. What was bugging him? Maybe if she could figure it out, then she could help him sort out his problem, and then maybe he'd really like her and pretty soon they'd be—

She sighed loudly.

Oh, who am I kidding, anyway?

Daley saw Eric rummaging through a pile of gear near the fire pit. It wasn't that she didn't trust him, but when she saw he had pulled out the only saw they had, she confronted him.

"What are you doing?" she asked.

"Well, what does it look like to you, Daley?"

"That belongs to the group," she said, pointing

at the saw. "You can't use it for your own shelter."

"Tell you what, Boss Lady." He gave her a snide smile. "There're seven of us here, right? So this is one-seventh mine. I'll be sure to use it for precisely one-seventh of the day."

He turned to walk off, but before he could go, Daley grabbed his arm.

"There's a little problem with your logic, Eric. If you've left the group, then you're not entitled to *any*thing that belongs to the group."

"Well, uh . . ." She could see the wheels going around in his head as he tried to come up with some kind of cheap rationalization. "Well, uh, I may have left the group in some ways, but not in others. How about that?"

"Not in others?" she repeated. "That's not quite what it sounded like a little while ago. Besides," she went on, "if you're intellectually committed to being a loner, then you can't just arbitrarily pick and choose. You can't be one of the group and *not* one of the group at the same time."

"Ooh," he mimicked, "in-tel-*lec*-tu-ally. Ar-bi-*trar*-i-ly! Wow! Your mental kung fu is so totally scaring me! But see, the thing is, I *am* here. I have the saw."

He held up the saw.

She looked at it angrily.

He waved it in her face. "Whatcha gonna do— take it from me?"

With that, he shook her hand off his arm, smirked, and sauntered off—saw in hand.

After his talk with Melissa, Jackson left the beach in hopes that a walk in the forest would help him know what to do. A few steps into the trees, though, and he realized he wasn't alone. The kid was standing there in the forest with a thoughtful expression on his face. Lex noticed Jackson and waved.

"Boy, am I glad to run into you, Jackson!" he called.

Something about Lex's enthusiasm made Jackson feel better. He was a lot easier to deal with than the older kids. In a lot of ways he was like Jackson—kind of wrapped up in his own world, not getting into everybody's business all the time.

"Hey, Lex," Jackson replied. "What's up?"

"Follow me. I've got to show you something."

"Oh?"

"Yeah. It's not far. It's something I started the day after the crash, but I didn't want to tell anybody about it, because if it didn't work, then, well—you know how they are most of the time."

Jackson shrugged. *Hey, why not?*

Lex led Jackson through the trees. It was obvious from the way the grass had been trampled that Lex had been on this little path a number of times before. Jackson had to admit, he was kind of intrigued. He'd noticed that Lex was always disappearing into the forest. But he hadn't given much thought to what the kid was doing.

Suddenly they came into a clearing, and Lex pointed down to the ground. Jackson looked where he was pointing, but it took him a second to actually see the tarp.

"What is it, Lex?"

"Look here," and he lifted up a corner of the tarp so Jackson could see.

Jackson stared for a long time, saying nothing.

"You don't like it?" Lex asked.

Jackson turned toward Lex and instead of a boy genius, he saw a little ten-year-old, looking for approval.

"Sure, Lex," he said. "It's good. It really is."

"I thought with everybody being so bummed right now, they'd like to know about it," Lex said softly.

Jackson peeked under the tarp again. Give the kid credit. He was thinking. But it crystallized something—a half-formed thought that had been brewing in the back of his mind for days . . . but that he just hadn't wanted to face.

"Thing is," Jackson said, "when I look at it, Lex, what I see is we're in bigger trouble than I thought."

After his face-off with Daley, Eric was feeling pumped.

This time he was gonna get it right. *I'm like the Shaolin monk going out into the wilderness, training in a solitary and unrelenting battle against mediocrity and weakness, turning myself into a hard, fierce warrior! Check out the master, you losers, 'cause your skills are garbage!*

He lost his train of thought as a sharp pain shot up his leg.

"Ow!" he shrieked. "Ow, ow, *owww!*"

He looked down to see what he'd walked into. It was the root of a dead palm tree. A big, strong-looking palm tree. As the pain subsided, a thought struck him. Lex had a point. Wood would be helpful. If he could saw this tree up, use it as the center pole of his teepee—man, that sucker wouldn't blow over in a Category 5 hurricane! Armed with the saw he had temporarily confiscated, he set to work on the tree, working away at the base. All he had to do was saw it free of this big ball of roots. Then he'd be golden! So maybe that brat had been right about his shelter not being very strong. No problem. This time he'd do it right.

'Cause there was no way he was gonna go crawling back to those goody-goodies. Not for a million bucks. No way, José.

Failure is not an option.

Just a little distance away, Taylor continued to sit, staring out at the ocean. Melissa walked by, surprised to see her still sitting there.

"Taylor?" she said. "Taylor, you haven't said much about what's going on. That's not like you."

Taylor remained mute, so still and quiet it gave Melissa the creeps.

"I wish you wouldn't ignore me," she went on. Still nothing.

"Taylor, this isn't funny. This really is not funny."

Melissa moved in closer to get a better look at Taylor's face. For the first time she could see Taylor's eyes. They were as empty as the calm blue water they reflected.

"Taylor."

No answer.

"Taylor!" Suddenly Melissa felt panicked. "Taylor? Are you okay? Taylor?"

Taylor just sat, wrapped in her sleeping bag, staring as though she could somehow absorb an understanding of what was wrong with her through the pulsing of the waves, the splash of the sea birds skimming across the surface of the water.

She wanted to get back with the others. She really did. She wanted to be making her video again. She really did. She wanted to understand why she felt so different from most of these other people. She really did.

But mostly she wanted to be home.

After the storm everything seemed so different, and she didn't know why, and she didn't know how to pull up out of this nosedive she was in. She figured Captain Russell, the pilot of their plane, must have felt the same way before the crash. Helpless. She wondered for a second where he and the other three kids were. But it was too hard. She just couldn't do it. It was as if she just kept heading down and down. She thought it might be nice to just get up and walk right into the ocean and keep on walking. Let it do whatever it would do. Because right now she felt like she might as well really be drowning.

She wished everyone would stop yakking at her. What were they going on about, anyway?

Why won't they shut up?

Eric was feeling pretty good about things. His shelter looked a lot better now. And once he put this tree trunk that he was cutting into the center of his shelter—dude, it would be like a fortress, a castle, a tower of architectural power! And the good news was that the trunk would fall nice and close to his shelter. So he wouldn't have to drag it very far.

And he was getting close. It seemed as if he'd been sawing for hours. But it ought to fall pretty soon. Not bad for working with just one dinky little saw. The wood was tougher than it looked, though, so the whole thing was taking a lot longer than he wished. But still. He had a pretty good notch sawed out of the tree now.

He straightened up, breathing hard, then shouted over to Taylor, "Don't listen to them, Taylor! If you want to sit and veg for a while, that's your right."

He sawed a little more. For some reason the saw started to jam. Was the wood swelling up, or what? He had to rock it back and forth a couple times for every cutting stroke. He was starting to get exhausted.

"Dude, don't let 'em beat you down," he called to Taylor. "Fight the power!" He held up his fist, shook it in the air, then winced. God! After all this sawing, it hurt just to make a fist.

Taylor didn't look up, didn't show any indication she even noticed he was there. Story of his life, huh? The honeys all took a rain check when it came to him.

Well, fine. But someday they'd see. Someday they'd get the picture. Eric McGorrill was not one of these losers who had to get permission to live his life. He was—

The saw slipped and nicked his hand. A thin

stream of blood oozed out of the wound. For a minute Eric felt totally alone. He stared at Taylor and a bitter expression crept onto his face.

Why can't she just look at me? That's all. Just one look? Is that so hard?

Meanwhile Jackson, Nathan, and Lex were at the fire pit listening to Daley.

"I don't want to say Eric's right," she said.

"No, of course not!" Nathan said.

"But it's clear what has to be done," she said. "We can all sleep in the same tent for a while, but that's gonna get old. Fast. And what *that* means is we're gonna *have* to have some kind of shelter. That storm tore the other tent to shreds, and another blow like that could rip up the only one we've got left."

"How about using the wing?" Nathan suggested.

"I don't know," she said. "I haven't thought about it enough. We need to get reorganized. Groups, you know?"

"Groups!" Nathan said. "Absolutely. Groups!" He cleared his throat. "Um. What kind of groups?"

"Work groups. One for finding more fruit, one for getting more fish—"

Suddenly Melissa appeared and burst into their conversation.

"We've got a problem!" she said.

"Gee," Nathan said. "You think?"

Melissa ignored his sarcasm. "It's Taylor," she said.

"What else is new?" Daley said, miffed at being interrupted.

"I'm serious. It's like she's in shock or something. She's totally nonfunctional. I mean, I was just down there trying to talk to her, and I got a look at her eyes. There's nothing there. Flat. There's just nobody home upstairs."

"That's not news." Nathan grunted.

"Nathan, this is not funny! I think that everything that happened last night must have pushed her over some kind of edge or whatever."

"She really hasn't said very much," Lex put in.

"Much? She hasn't said anything. Nada. Nothing. Not since the storm."

"You're right," Daley said. "That *is* weird."

They all sat still, looking now and then at one another to see if anyone had a handle on what to do. What they did understand was that this was way beyond any of their realms of experience.

It was Nathan who finally put it into a question.

"What should we do?" he asked.

No one had noticed that the rasping sound of Eric's saw had been still for a while until they saw him standing right at the edge of their group.

"Nothing," Eric nearly screamed. "Why do you feel obliged to freakin' butt in every time somebody has a problem? Just leave her alone! The best thing in the world you can do is stop trying to run people's lives! Why do you think I'm building my own shelter? To get away from all the pressure to do things *your* way."

"But she's really hurting," Melissa said. "Eric, you haven't looked in her face."

"I still say she'll be fine if all of you'd just stop trying to tell her what to do," Eric insisted.

"Jackson," Daley said, "We're falling apart here. You have to do something."

Everyone stared at Jackson.

"You're right," he finally said. "We *are* falling apart. Everybody's got their own little agenda. Everybody's got their own little opinion."

"So what's *your* opinion?" Daley asked.

"Opinion?" He was quiet for just a second, then he got to his feet and looked each kid in the eyes. "I'm gonna go check on Taylor for you."

He began walking away.

"Yeah, but Jackson, you're the leader," Daley said. "We need to decide—"

He stopped and turned back to the group.

"All right, I'm just gonna say it. I'm sick of all the drama. Congratulations, Daley. You're the new leader. I resign."

With that, he left the circle to make his way down toward the shoreline where Taylor kept her silent vigil.

FO_UR

Daley

Daley here again. I can't believe I yelled at Taylor for being lazy. I didn't realize how much she was hurting. And now Jackson's bailed on being leader and wants me to take over. It's what I wanted from the start, but . . . I don't know. Am I up for this?

And what do we do about Taylor? We can't just leave her hanging. Can we? We have to help her some way. Don't we? Eric thinks we're trying to run everybody's lives or something. But we just want to help. But to really help, you have to have a plan.

Right?

Jackson passed Eric—who was over on the other side of the tree line, sawing half-heartedly at a log—then approached Taylor. She didn't move.

"Hey," Jackson said finally.

Taylor didn't make any motion for him to sit or even give any indication that she wanted him to talk. But he sat down next to her anyway.

"Having any fun yet?" he asked gently, not really expecting her to respond. "I gotta tell you this, Taylor: Nobody here is as strong or as brave as they pretend to be. Not a single one of us. I know you take a lot of grief. Of course you're pretty good at handing it out, too." He laughed softly. "But I'll tell you something else. I think you're the only one here who's being totally honest. Man, I gotta respect that."

He sat quietly for a moment.

"Listen, if you ever do want to talk about things, try me. I mean it. I don't judge people. At least I wouldn't judge you, because I know where you're coming from. I really think I do."

Funny, he thought. She came from the richest, most privileged background of anybody here. And he came from the poorest. And yet he had a feeling they had something in common. From what little he'd heard around the school, Taylor barely ever saw her dad. He was flying all over the world making money. And her mom? Sounded like she was a rich version of his own mom—a little too fond of the happy pills, a little too wrapped up in all her own stupid dramas to pay any attention to her own kid.

Jackson was going to touch her arm with a little reassuring pat, but thought better of it. Once again, Eric was probably right. Probably the best thing he could do was just leave her alone. He got up quietly and walked away.

As Jackson left, Taylor looked up and stared after him.

She felt something, but wasn't sure what it was. Something that kind of scared her.

Daley and Nathan found themselves at the wing. Daley watched while Nathan scurried around, poking and prodding and testing things.

Finally he said, "It's pretty solid, Daley. I think it might do as a wall somehow. What do you think?"

But Daley didn't say anything. She was trying to concentrate on the whole shelter-building issue, but she couldn't. She was worried about all these random thoughts she kept having. About Nathan.

This is not like me, she kept telling herself. *It's not like me to be second-guessing myself so much.*

Then she felt Nathan tapping gently on her forehead.

"Hello," he said. "Anybody home?"

"Oh," she answered. "I'm sorry. Yeah, that sounds like a good idea—what you were saying. About the wing?"

"Daley, are you okay?"

"Oh, I don't know, Nathan. I was thinking about Jackson. He wasn't exactly Mr. Perfect as a leader, but at least he gave us a kind of structure. We're bound to get even more unraveled now, more scattered."

"Well, then do what he said, Daley. Take over."

"That isn't funny, Nathan."

"Daley, read my lips: I'm not trying to be funny."

"You mean you don't still want to be leader? You were all about that when we got here."

Nathan was silent for a minute. Finally he said, "I want what's best for everybody, and maybe I can get more done by helping you than by being the leader."

She looked directly at him, looking for even a hint that he was slinging BS, that he was waiting to unleash some kind of zinger. But there was no sign of it. He seemed strangely sincere.

Her face took on a slightly harder look, the skepticism apparent in her voice. "So, you're really saying you *want* me to be the leader?"

"It's a no-brainer, Daley. You actually *like* all this organization crap. Who could do it better? Well, with me backing you up, of course."

"Omigod!" she said, her eyes wide in mock horror. "Where's Nathan? What have you done with him?"

He chuckled.

"Okay, what changed?" she asked.

"A lot of things, actually. Come on," and he started marching off like a man on a mission.

Curious, Daley followed him.

They strode past Eric, who was making good progress at sawing up his tree. He looked up and grimaced, but said nothing and made no move to join them. But as they marched past the fire pit where Melissa was getting the fire going again, Nathan motioned for her to join them. She looked questioningly at Daley, who gave her a "don't ask me" shrug. She put down the water pail in her hand and followed them.

"*Lex!*" Nathan yelled. "Where's Lex? *Lex!*" he shouted again. "Come down to the tent, Lex. We're gonna have a powwow."

After a moment Lex emerged from the woods—back from whatever mysterious place he kept wandering off to. Jackson showed up at the fire pit hauling jugs of water. As Nathan passed him, he said, "Come with me."

Jackson eyed the little parade, then set down his water jugs and followed them.

"Eric," Nathan hollered out. "We're having a meeting."

"A meeting? Oh, goody," he hollered back. "Make sure not to start before I get there, now. I don't want to miss a single exciting word." He started sawing with renewed fury.

Nathan spotted Taylor, who still sat at the fire pit. She was still detached as she had been. But he walked over to her.

"What's happening?" Lex panted as he followed the others.

"I'm calling a meeting," Nathan answered. "Taylor's here, so we'll have it here. Get comfortable, everybody. This may take a while."

The others found places to sit while Nathan continued to stand.

"What about Eric?" Melissa asked.

"You coming, Eric?" Nathan hollered up toward Eric.

There was no answer from Eric, who made a big show of sawing hard.

"So what's this all about?" Jackson asked.

Daley had been wondering the same thing.

As partial answer, Nathan pointed up toward Eric and his tree.

"It's about what he's doing. And about all of us."

Standing in the center of the group, and slowly circling, Nathan started to speak. As he moved, he looked at each person in turn. He spoke clearly, with purpose, and with an authority that surprised Daley.

"Let's get it out on the table right away: We've been lost for, like, two weeks now. We don't know what's going to happen. Nobody's found us." He paused at that for a brief moment. "But they will. I believe that. It might be sooner, it might be later, but we . . . will . . . be . . . found. Our *only* job is to stay alive until that happens. It's as simple as that."

Daley felt an odd shiver run through her. She wished she could be as confident as he was. But it didn't sound like silly posing. He sounded like somebody you could believe. Somebody you could count on. Somebody you could trust. Somebody—

Okay, okay, okay! Daley told herself. *Knock it off. He's a good guy, but no need to get all goofy just because he makes a good speech.*

"We've survived a plane crash," Nathan continued. "We've found food and water. We've been through sickness and storms and injuries and bugs—and we're still here. You know why?" He surveyed the group again. "Because we all play a part. At one time or another we've all messed up, but somebody was always there to pick up the slack. We can complain all we want, but the bottom line is we need each other."

The circle was silent.

Even Eric had stopped sawing on his tree. Daley glanced at him. He had a look of bogus concentration on his face, as though he was studying the tree. But it was obvious he was eavesdropping.

"Every choice we make," Nathan was saying, "affects us all. We don't always agree, but that's why we need somebody to keep us focused. We've been calling that person a leader, but that person is really just a referee. Jackson doesn't want to be that person. That's cool. His choice. Don't blame him. But we still need somebody—*not* to be the boss, *not* to be in charge, but to help keep us from spinning out of control. I think it's pretty obvious there's only one person who can do that."

He paused and looked squarely at Daley. She felt her face flush.

"But this isn't about looking to somebody to tell us what to do. We *all* have to take responsibility for the group. If we don't, it won't matter how long it takes for our rescuers to come, because we won't be here to welcome them. It's as simple as that. If we don't stand together, we're going to die alone. And I, for one, am not into dying."

When they realized he was through, the others slowly looked around at each other. They didn't know what was supposed to happen next, what they were supposed to do next.

There was a long silence. Then Eric's saw began rasping away again.

Finally Jackson stood up and nodded to Nathan. Then Lex got up and stood by Jackson. Quickly, then, Melissa was up by Lex and Nathan. Last, Daley stood, smiling. Then, remembering there was still another person to consider, they all looked over at Taylor, who had never moved. Nathan was about to say something to her, but—

"Timberrrrr!"

It was Eric.

They whirled around just in time to see the tree he had been sawing start its downward path.

Eric ducked to one side, but it was falling toward him. For a moment he stood stock-still, a look of surprise on his face. He seemed to have misjudged where it was going to fall. He ducked to the other side. The tree slowly, slowly tipped over, letting out a loud cracking, crunching, popping noise, like some giant had dumped milk on a bowl of jumbo Rice Krispies.

"No," Eric hollered. "No, no, no!"

Why's he so upset? Daley wondered. He was safe now, out of the tree's path.

Then she saw it.

"Nooo!" Eric's voice was frantic. It all seemed to happen in slow motion. The tree—falling, falling, falling . . .

. . . directly on top of his shelter.

"NOOOOO!!"

With a horrible shattering, clattering crunch,

Eric's shelter was crushed into a billion pieces.

In the long silence that followed, Eric simply stood there, eyes trained on the wreckage that had been his shelter. His face went blank.

Everybody stared silently.

And then, suddenly, breaking into the moment, they heard a hysterical cry.

At first, Daley thought somebody was hurt. Was it Eric? But no, the sound was behind her.

And after a second she realized it wasn't a cry, but a howl of laughter. Who in the world could be laughing at a time like this?

She turned and saw—

"Taylor?" But Taylor didn't answer. She had flopped backward on the sand, her head thrown back, her mouth open wide, her arms clutching her stomach as peal after peal of laughter poured from her.

"Taylor?" Daley repeated. "Are you okay?"

Finally Taylor recovered enough to sit up. She looked around the group, then pointed at the wreckage of Eric's teepee.

"Now *that*," Taylor finally managed to say, "*that* is what I call funny."

Jackson's face lit up with an uncharacteristic grin.

He turned, looked around the ring, and said, "Cool. She's back."

FIVE

ater that day, after Eric's disaster and Taylor's recovery, Lex was leading the entire group along his trail through the jungle. He was in high spirits, chatting all the while. Taylor was right behind him.

"I guarantee," Lex said, "everybody's gonna love this."

"If there's not a pizza involved, I doubt it," Taylor said, then yelled out in pain as her foot rolled over on a branch. She hopped awkwardly, grabbing at her ankle.

"What'd you do, Lex, set out booby traps or something? This better be worth it."

Nathan and Daley were walking side by side, and Nathan whispered, "I have to admit, I liked it better when Taylor wasn't talking."

After a bit more walking, they came to Lex's tarp. They all gathered around it expectantly.

"See," Lex explained, "I was afraid the storm might have washed it away, but it was protected. I'd seen to that, and I didn't lose a thing."

Lex sensed that they were impatient to see what he'd dragged them out here for. But he couldn't help himself: He had to explain some details about the work he'd been doing so they'd understand he hadn't been out here goofing off all this time.

"Wow," Taylor said. "Like, that's the best-looking chunk of plastic I've ever seen. Thanks, junior. I couldn't wait to get here, and a twisted ankle is nothing to pay for looking at this."

She started to go, but Jackson stopped her. "Wait, Taylor. Give him a minute."

"I started this," Lex explained, "right after the plane crashed, but I didn't want to show it to you guys until I knew it was going to work."

He reached down to the tarp. "It won't be long before we've got our own source . . . of food!" and with that he pulled the tarp all the way off, grinning proudly.

They all looked down and saw a garden. It was bordered by logs on the ground, marking off an area about twelve by twelve feet. There were six-inch-high shoots of new growth in neat rows.

They all looked in wonder, smiles sprouting to match the growth on the ground.

"A vegetable garden," he said, feeling a rush of excitement at the looks of amazement on the older kids' faces. "We've got tomatoes, squash, melons, corn, and even potatoes and carrots."

"Lex, this is awesome!" Melissa said.

"But, Lex, where did you get the seeds?" Nathan asked.

"Mostly from the packages of food we brought, but I found some things growing wild right around here."

"Wait a minute," Eric said. "You mean you planted a tomato, and we're going to get, like, more tomatoes?"

Lex frowned. Was Eric really that dumb? Or was he just making some kind of joke? "Well, yeah, Eric, that's how it's always worked. I mean, tomatoes get *sold* in grocery stores, but they don't *grow* them there."

"That's like magic," Taylor put in.

"Lex," said Daley, "this is just flat-out amazing. How long before we get fruit?"

The truth was, Lex wasn't entirely sure. "Depends on the plant, I guess," he said. "They're all pretty fast-growing in this kind of climate, so we might start seeing something in a month or so."

Everyone was smiling at this sudden, unexpected garden of plenty, this gift of life and hope, this quiet intrusion of normality into their lives. If this could happen . . .

But the euphoria drained out of their faces as they started to connect some dots, started to understand what else was at stake.

"So, the good news," Nathan said slowly, wanting to put the best possible face on the moment, "is that we'll have a regenerating food supply in about a month."

"Yeah," Jackson answered quietly. "And the bad news is, if we can't find some more food in the meantime, we might not be here to eat it."

With that, they looked at one another, trying hard to side with Nathan but knowing they had to accept Jackson's vision as well.

"So," said Daley, more to herself than anyone in particular as she balanced the two truths. "Hope for the best, prepare for the worst, like they say."

They all knew she was right, but the worst certainly looked like the winner right then.

But Lex wasn't worried. They'd think of something. They always had.

Nathan

Lex is one smart kid. A garden is a great idea—I should have thought of that . . . All of us should have thought of that.

SIX

Taylor lay in the tent, sleepless and irritated. Here they were, all jammed into this icky little tent that was made for maybe three people. She felt Daley's elbow in her back, somebody's head on her feet—whose? And—*total* gross-out!—somebody's stinky feet were about two inches from her face. And then nobody could really take baths, so everybody— except *her*, of course—smelled like armpit.

Gross! Gross! *Gross!*

And then Lex had to be *reading*. He had a flashlight in his mouth directed at his book. Taylor fixated on Lex's flashlight, on it's every wobble and jiggle, on the weird shadows it cast, on the fact that there was probably drool running down the side of it.

Gross!

"Daley," she finally called out in a stage whisper. "Are you asleep?"

"Yes," Daley answered.

"Well, I'm not," Melissa replied. "Not anymore, at least."

It wasn't fair that everybody else got to sleep and Taylor didn't. If she couldn't sleep, hey, *nobody* was gonna sleep. Still in her stage whisper, she called out to anyone who would listen. "Tell Lex to put out that light. I can't sleep."

"You tell him," Melissa whispered back.

"Besides, it's disgusting. He has it in his mouth. I might have to touch it someday."

"Whatever," somebody else whispered.

No longer even pretending to whisper, Taylor belted out, "Hey, peewee. Go to sleep!"

At that, Eric sat bolt upright. "What!" he called out, surprised, awake. "What? What!"

Which woke Nathan, who jumped violently in his small slot on the floor. "Ow," he screamed. "Ouch! Toenails, whose toenails? Something's trying to claw me to death."

Which caused Eric to turn over quickly, kneeing Jackson in the process, who also sat up hollering, "Who kicked me? Somebody kneed me."

With that, everybody started sitting up, calling out, muttering in their groggy efforts to fathom what was going on. Taylor felt a little better now.

At least she wasn't alone in her extreme misery.

"Oh, go to sleep, everybody," said Melissa.

"Well, I'm trying," Eric said.

"Try outside, then," said Nathan.

"It happens to be pouring rain," Eric said.

"So, what's happening?" Daley asked no one in particular.

"I can't sleep with that light on," Taylor said.

"Then *you* sleep outside," Eric shot back.

"And not that I want to point fingers," Taylor said, pointing her finger toward Eric's voice in the dark, "but you stink."

"Taylor!" Melissa chided

"What!" she shot back. "He does stink."

"That's cool," Eric said. "I'll just move over here, then."

Eric stood, but in trying to move he stepped on Lex, tripped, fell, and crashed into the tent, causing it to cave in on that side.

Suddenly the tent was filled with screaming and general confusion. Lex's flashlight beam flailed all over the place as he tried to focus it on whatever seemed most reasonable to help things get straight again, but the disorder was universal—everyone shouted questions and orders, but nobody paid much attention to anyone else.

Nathan, however, did manage to stand up and grab the pole that had been knocked askew. He set it back into the ground.

"Shut up!" Nathan screamed over the rest of the noise.

For just a moment there was nothing but the sound of a now fairly gentle rain on the tent.

"Oh, man. We just gotta get a bigger tent," Nathan muttered.

Over their own murmurs, they tried to rearrange themselves back into their cramped slots. It was like solving a jigsaw puzzle, trying to get everybody to fit again. Everybody—except Taylor, who had seized the opportunity to grab herself an extra three or four inches of space—grumbled and moaned and sighed, their sleep completely ruined.

Much better, Taylor thought, smiling. Then, she lay her head back down and began to snore.

Daley looked around the group as they huddled near the miserable fire that Jackson had started at dawn. Everybody looked irritable—stretching to unkink their muscles, yawning after their sleepless night, rubbing their hands against the morning chill.

Nobody spoke.

Finally Taylor looked around and said, "I love you people. Truly I do, but sleeping in that—that *thing* won't do." She pointed at the miserable-looking tent. "It won't. Not at all. It just isn't *right.*"

Daley nodded. She'd been thinking exactly the same thing. "I know," she put in. "It's true, and what we've got to do is build a shelter. One for the guys and one for us."

"That's *two* shelters," Eric noted. He held up his hands, which were covered with blisters from working on his failed house. "Frankly, I don't think my hands could even make *one* shelter right now."

"One shelter, one tent," Nathan suggested.

"I call dibs on the tent," Taylor said, quick to get her bid in first.

"We can build something by the fire, where it'll be nice and warm at night," Lex added.

"Oh," Taylor said. "Dibs on the shelter."

"But there aren't any trees here," Melissa put in. "Don't we need trees for protection?"

"Lotta good it did before," Eric muttered.

"Well, wherever we build it, it's going to be tough making it comfortable," Daley said.

"Dibs on the tent," Taylor chimed in again.

"I like sleeping on sand," Melissa said.

"But a shelter won't be sealed like a tent," said Lex. "We'd have to build it raised off the ground."

"That's a lot of work," said Jackson.

"Too much," Eric grumbled. He held up his blistered hands again.

"And it's got to stand up to another storm," Nathan added.

"So let's build a platform," Melissa said.

"I thought you liked the sand," Eric reminded her.

"It's gotta be near the fire, or it'll get real cold," Lex reminded them again.

"Then why can't we put the fire over where we build the shelter?" Daley asked.

"I call dibs on the shelter," Taylor said.

"Fire under the trees?" Jackson objected. "That's not real smart."

"Dibs on the tent," Taylor managed to get in again.

"Well, just who do you think is gonna build this thing, anyway?" Eric protested.

And they were suddenly all talking at once: one-on-one, two-on-two, until no one could hear anything that anyone else was saying. Daley looked around at the confused group. It was obvious nobody was listening to anybody. She sighed. *Why does it always come down to me to get the group rowing in the same direction?*

"Hey! Whoa!" she yelled, and held up her hands to get their attention. "Wait a sec! Hold on!"

Slowly they all fell into a silence.

All except Taylor: "I call dibs on the ... wait ..." She looked around the circle of faces and blinked. "What are we doing now?"

"Arguing, as usual," Daley said. "Guys, we just can't let every single thing we have to discuss turn into a fight."

"Okay, Miss New Boss," said Eric. "So tell me what to do."

"It's not about me telling you what to do," said Daley, exasperated. "It's about figuring out what's right. What *needs* to be done."

"We should be more like ants," said Lex.

Lex, as usual, full of weird ideas. Everybody stared blankly at him.

Lex opened his mouth as though to explain, but Melissa spoke first. "Yeah, Daley, but how do we figure out what's right when everybody has a different opinion?"

"Well," she said, playing for time, praying for an idea. "Well, let's try something new. How about this? Um, how about voting?"

"Voting? That's not exactly a never-before-heard-of concept," Eric pointed out.

"Sure it is," Daley shot back. "When we voted before it was to elect a leader."

"Hey," Nathan said. His face had brightened up, his eyes shining. "That's a great idea. Look, this is about everybody having a say in what happens. It's like, you know, a democracy."

"And," Melissa quickly joined in, "there're seven of us, so there can't be any ties."

"Exactly," Daley chimed in. "And if it works, we can do it every time there's an issue. Who's up for it?"

Melissa raised her hand, then Nathan, Lex, Daley, then all the rest.

"Unanimous," Daley almost screamed. "Now see? That wasn't so hard, was it?"

"But all we did was vote to vote," said Taylor.

"So now what do we vote on? How to vote?"

"No," Daley answered. "It's simple. Look. Who's in favor of building another shelter?"

All of them slowly raised their hands.

"Done! So where's it gonna be built?" Daley continued. "Who says by the fire?"

At that, Daley, Melissa, Jackson, Lex, and Nathan raised their hands.

"Five out of seven," Daley said. "Done! We build it here. Now, do we build on sand for comfort or off the ground to stay dry? Who says sand?"

Nathan, Eric, and Taylor raised their hands.

"Who says off the ground?"

Daley, Lex, Jackson, and Melissa raised their hands.

"Done!" Daley was excited. This was working great! "Four to three. We build a platform. Who sleeps in it? Boys or girls?"

"Wait up there," said Taylor. "That's not fair. They have one more than us."

"You're right," said Daley, now feeling a rush from leading her little band through the snares and traps of decision-making at this basic level. "Any debate?"

Melissa furrowed her brow just a little. "Daley, don't you think we should build the shelter before we decide who's gonna be sleeping in it?"

"Okay. Who agrees with Melissa?"

At that they all raised their hands.

"Done!" said Daley. "Wow!" It was amazing how quickly they were accomplishing things now.

No pointless debate, no whining and complaining. Just vote and move on.

Then Taylor said, "I still have dibs on ... well ... whatever," she finished lamely.

"People," Daley called out. "People, we've just made ourselves a democracy!"

At that, they all looked around at each other, trading high fives and knuckle raps.

"Wait a minute," Lex suddenly called out.

"What?" Daley asked.

"Well, we never voted on something. I mean, we voted on something, but there weren't enough choices."

"What?" Daley asked again.

"When we were voting on where to build the shelter. There were only two choices: by the fire or closer to the trees."

"Right, squirt," said Eric, "and you voted for the fire."

"Yeah, I know. But we were going awfully fast, and there's something we didn't consider. I mean, what about having to build it on the flattest ground? This beach slopes in all kinds of directions."

"Well . . ." Daley was a little annoyed at this interruption of her smoothly functioning decision-making machine. "Well, let's revote and include that. Everybody cool with that?"

"Then what's the point of voting in the first place?" Taylor asked.

"Yeah," Eric piped up. "If we vote, we vote. Are

you telling us that all this means is anybody can make us vote again just because he wasn't bright enough the first time?"

"It's not a matter of being bright, Eric," Nathan put in. "We're all 'bright enough' to vote, but Lex raised a good point, it seems to me."

"But what about the democratic process, dude?" Eric said, eyebrows raised.

"Whoa," Jackson offered. "Two different things going on here: One's preference, the other's technical."

"Right," Nathan confirmed. "Our votes were for what we preferred. We preferred to build down near the fire. But if that's not the best construction site for building reasons, then we have to change our plans. We're still not changing a *preference* vote. We're just noting that there're lots of things you can't know until you get started on something."

"Huh?" Eric said. "Technical? Preference? I'm getting lost."

"Yeah, if the voting doesn't decide anything, what's the point of even doing it?" Taylor asked again. "All it does is take up time, and I have better things to do with my life. My hair needs washing big-time!"

"Good grief, Taylor," Daley said, sensing that she needed to get things back in order. "As I recall, you were the one who noticed that the girls were outnumbered by the boys. And Melissa noted that we ought to get the thing built before we decide who's gonna be in it. Now Lex brought up another point."

"After we voted, though," insisted Eric.

"Well, it's still a technical point, not a preference point—as Jackson pointed out," Daley repeated. "I mean, we're not trying to rush the voting."

Jackson looked off into the air. "Could have fooled me," he said softly.

Lex

Hello! Can anyone hear me? Can anyone see me?

Just as I thought—I'M INVISIBLE. I know the big kids mean well, but they never pay attention to me. And I have good ideas, too—I was the one who planted a garden, and figured out how to hook up the speakers, and fixed the radio—before it washed away. They even listen to Taylor more than they listen to me . . . It's just not fair.

After the meeting, Jackson noticed that Lex just seemed to be hanging around, doing nothing. Which was unlike the kid. He sat on a fallen palm tree, staring at the wood.

So Jackson sidled nearer and waited just a little before saying anything to him.

"Ants?" Jackson finally said quietly.

Lex turned. "Hey, Jackson." Then he looked down at the palm tree again.

"Ants?" Jackson repeated.

"Aw, I don't know. That's what I was reading about last night in the tent before Taylor got everybody all stirred up."

"Taylor's okay, Lex. She's kinda different. She sees her own world and doesn't think much about other people. But she's good. She's got game."

"If you say so, Jackson." Lex didn't look up.

"But what about the ants? You said we should be more like ants."

"Yeah, well, that's when Daley was trying to get everybody not to think about being told what to do, but to just do the right thing or whatever. And it just seemed like we'd be better off around here if we were more like ants."

He paused as he looked up at Jackson.

"You know anything about ants, Jackson?"

"Nope, not really, Lex. They live in colonies. If they're carpenter ants, they can eat your house up. If they're red ants, they can bite and give you itchy welts. They're pests in the kitchen, and they're not welcome at picnics. Otherwise . . ." He shrugged his shoulders.

"Look," Lex said, "check this out." He pointed at the wood he'd been staring at.

Jackson looked closer. A thin trail of tiny ants

was moving across the surface of the palm tree.

"Well," Lex started, "you're right about their living in colonies, and they've also got queen ants—just like queen bees in beehives. But the thing about ants is they don't have any leaders. Look at them." He pointed again. The ants were carrying little bits of white stuff, all of them scurrying quickly along the wood. "They've got thousands and thousands of ants in their nests but nobody telling them what to do. I mean, they can't talk. They can't write. They can't make speeches or vote."

"And?"

"Well, the queen doesn't do anything except lay eggs. Every now and then a couple of ants grow wings and head out. Then another bunch of ants grow wings, and chase them and fertilize them, and then they die, I think, and the queen goes off and starts another colony. But that's all she does. Lay eggs."

"Okay."

"But think of all the things ants *do*."

"Like?"

"They build very complex nests. They capture other ants and make them slaves. They capture other ants and milk them. Whenever they somehow know it'll rain, they build earthworks around the entrance holes to their nests so that rising water won't flow in. They colonize. And they do all this cool stuff without any leaders. They just seem to know what to do."

"They *know*?" Jackson asked. "Do ants have brains?"

"Not like we do, no. They just *do* all this stuff. They somehow just *know* what has to be done. And then they *do* it."

Jackson nodded, seeing what he was getting at. "No votes? No arguments?"

"Nothing like that. I guess that's what I was thinking, Jackson. Wouldn't it be great if we could just do it like that? Like, if you know what needs to be done, then just go do it."

They were both very quiet for a time.

Then Jackson said, "Lex, you're quite a guy, you know?"

Lex looked down at the beach right near him. "Yeah, but who cares? Nobody ever listens to me." He reached out and swatted the trail of ants. Hundreds of the tiny insects flew off into the sand. It didn't seem to bother them, though. They immediately went back to work, forming a new trail.

Jackson said nothing. They sat in silence for a while.

"Hey, Jackson. If you're not into ants, you'll love this."

"What's that, Lex?"

"Fireflies. There're some really, really cool kinds of fireflies out here in the South Pacific."

But Jackson raised one hand, palm forward, toward Lex.

"Not now, Lex. Not today. Later on, buddy."

SEVEN

It was that dead time that comes between the decision to get started on a project and gearing up for the actual work. Eric had already been kicking back at the beach to get some rays, but he had gotten a little too hot, so he picked up his salvaged airplane chair and dragged it into some shade closer to the tree line. He was only partly facing the ocean, so there was mainly the tangle of trees, vines, and other growth in his line of vision, but something caught his eye. It was a dull glare reflecting from something that seemed to be buried in the sand.

He stared at it for a long time, off and on, before his curiosity was piqued enough to make him get out of his chair. He slowly made his way toward whatever it was, not excited enough to hurry, but not disinterested enough to stay away from it, either.

When he was standing right next to it, he studied it for just a few seconds, then knelt to get a closer look. It seemed familiar but also strange—a little unusual but not exactly odd.

It was clearly metal, and judging from the one corner he could see, not very big. The rest of it was buried in the sand, which he started to brush away. Soon he was digging in earnest. It was solidly buried, and Eric worked up a sweat to get it loose. His hands still ached from all the sawing yesterday. But he was curious enough that he kept at it.

He yanked and heaved.

With a sucking sound, the entire thing popped free of the sand. He fell backward in a heap.

When he sat up, there it was, lying on the sand.

It was a box. Metal, painted olive green, with a dappled look and feel to it. The paint on the exposed corner was somewhat worn away and the texture had been rubbed down.

He looked around to see if anybody had noticed him. If it was something cool, he'd definitely want to keep it for himself.

Nobody was paying any attention to him.

Turning it over carefully, he saw that the box was tightly closed with metal snap hinges on either side. It was maybe a foot long and about five or six inches wide—about the volume of a shoebox, but not that shape at all. There was also

a handle on top. Then it hit him. He had seen
boxes like this in all those old war movies his dad
watched on the corny TV channels that you had
to flip past to get to MTV: It was an ammunition
box. An ammunition box from World War II.

"Whoa," Eric said to himself. "I wonder if
there's any ammo still in it."

It would stink to come all this way—only to get
shot when a bunch of ancient bullets exploded
by accident.

He shook his find gently back and forth a
few times. It wasn't all that heavy, so he figured
it didn't have anything in it. Not belts or clips of
ammunition, anyway. Still, he could hear and feel
something shuffling inside.

"Whoa," he said again.

Then he looked around again, carefully
scanning the area for signs that any of the others
might have noticed him digging around. This
was going to be *his* box. No Daley-organizing-
Nathan-schmoozing-Jackson-glowering sharing
with *this* baby. No way, dude.

His need to open the thing was almost more
than he could stand, but he decided against it.
Anything could be in that box, and besides, he
didn't want to open it out here on the beach,
because what*ever* was in there was *his*.

He wrapped it in his shirt, which he had taken
off when he was tanning himself, then started
back to his private pile of stuff in the tent, hoping

no one would be there before he could figure out where to hide the box.

Back at the other end of the beach, Melissa and Nathan were brushing sand off the wing of the plane.

"We definitely want to keep the sand and stuff off it," Nathan said. "It'll reflect the sun better if we do, and any planes up there looking for us will see it better."

"Do you think we should use it for the shelter?" Melissa asked.

"I don't know." Nathan had been thinking about that question for a while. But he wasn't quite sure what they could do with it. It was long but not very wide. Too thin for a roof, too short and oddly shaped for a wall. "It might be better to leave it out here where it can be seen."

"Hey! Maybe we should vote on it?"

They both laughed.

"Funny," Nathan said. "But you know, that really was pretty amazing how Daley stepped up."

Melissa nodded. "Yeah, I think things are gonna be a lot easier now. Maybe we all needed to blow off steam so we could start over, try it again."

"You bet," Nathan said, then paused, not quite sure if he should go on and say what he had been thinking about. "A new beginning, Mel. That's why I'm going to go on and tell Daley how I feel about her."

"Wow! Seriously?"

"It's too hard keeping it secret, Mel. I'm gonna do it." Nathan felt better the second the words came out of his mouth. "I'm gonna tell her how much I really like her."

"You don't think it will make things kinda weird?"

"Well, it could. But it's weirder not being straight up about it. I just have to be honest with her, like you said."

Melissa reached over and put her hand on his arm. "You're doing the right thing," she said.

"You really think so?"

"I do."

"Well, check in with me after I tell her."

Eric

Why can't everyone just mind their own business? I found the box—it's mine. End of story. And I'm not sharing it with those losers anyway. So they'll just have to get over it.

Eric had just about gotten his secret box hidden under a pile of shirts when Taylor blew into the tent.

"Whew! I have *so* been working," she announced.

Eric turned quickly away from her, trying frantically to pretend he wasn't hiding something.

"Hey," she said. "What's that?"

Just as she asked the question, Lex appeared in the door of the tent.

"Cool," Lex said. "Yeah, what *is* that?"

"He was trying to hide it," Taylor said smugly to the younger boy.

"I was not!" Eric tried to act innocent. "It's nothing. It's just something that was on the plane."

At which point Melissa walked into the tent and looked right at the ammo box. "*What* was on the plane?" she said.

"Huh?" Eric said. "Oh ... uh ... this."

"No, it wasn't," Melissa said.

"Huh? What?" Eric was still doing his best to act bewildered.

"That box." Melissa pointed. "That box was not on the plane. I know because I helped Daley inventory all our stuff."

"Look," Eric said, lowering his voice. "Okay, forget it. So it wasn't on the plane. Big deal. It's mine."

"Well, why is it so precious?" Taylor asked.

"*I* found it," Eric said. "That's why."

"So keep it," Lex said. "But what is it?"

Eric knew he couldn't pretend anymore, so he brought it out into plain sight.

"Oh, *wow*," Taylor said sarcastically. "A box."

"Excellent!" Lex almost whispered in his awe at

what he was looking at. "Do you know what that is, Eric?"

"I've got a pretty good idea." Eric didn't like having some ten-year-old lecturing him.

"It's an ammo box," said Lex. "I'll bet it's from the Second World War. What do you suppose is in it?"

"Ammo?" Taylor said. "What's ammo?"

Before anyone had a chance to answer, Jackson walked into the tent. His eyes went straight to the box.

"Boy, that looks pretty old," Jackson said.

"You too?" Eric clutched the box to his chest. "For a deserted island this place has sure gotten awfully crowded."

"Is it a radio?" Melissa asked, her voice suddenly sounding truly hopeful.

"It's an ammo box," Lex said.

"Who cares!" Eric shouted. "It's *mine.*"

"Well, what are you going to do with it?" Jackson wanted to know.

Now there was a circle of kids staring at his box. After a moment of silence, Eric grabbed the camp knife and got ready to attack the box.

"Wait!" yelled Lex. "Wait! There's no telling what's in that thing. There could be a bomb. Or a live grenade. Even old ammunition can be unstable. It might explode."

At that, Taylor screamed and dived out the door into the sand, Melissa scooted as far from it as she could, and Jackson looked worried.

Eric hesitated, the knife held in his fist over the box. A live grenade? That would be even worse than getting shot. He imagined lying on the ground for days with all these little holes in his body, his blown-off legs and arms scattered all around the sand, flies crawling on his—

"Let's at least take it outside the tent," Jackson suggested. "We don't want it to blow up until we get the shelter built."

Eric sighed. "All right," he said. *"All right!"* He grabbed the box and raced out through the tent's flap. Then he yelled at the top of his lungs:

"COME DOWN TO THE TENT! COME DOWN TO THE TENT! THIS TIME *I'M* CALLING A MEETING! COME DOWN TO THE TENT!"

Nathan had drawn a sketchy outline of their beach in the sand near the fire pit. He had marked off some of the contours of the shore and where—roughly—the plane wing, the fire pit, the tent, and Lex's garden were, when Daley showed up with some gathered firewood.

"What's up?" Daley asked, dumping the wood next to the fire.

"Oh, just trying to figure out where the shelter might go."

"We've already voted on that, Nathan. Remember?"

Truth was, he didn't really care where the

shelter went. He scratched around a little more, trying to work up his courage to tell Daley of his feelings for her, but her being there—right *there*—unnerved him so much, he felt like running away and just forgetting the whole thing. But now that he'd made the decision to talk to her . . .

"Daley . . ." he started, wondering if his voice was cracking.

She looked at him curiously. "What, Nathan?"

"This may sound kinda weird—but there's something I've been meaning to talk to you about."

"All right," she said.

He hesitated. Then, while he was still thinking, a racket came from over near the tent. Eric, shouting something about a meeting.

"What in the world?" Daley said. They looked at each other. *Eric* calling a meeting?

"This I have to see," Nathan said, halfway relieved to have been interrupted. They both dropped everything and ran down the beach toward the tent.

When they got there they saw the others sitting around in a circle. Eric stood in the center holding something carefully in his hands.

"What's happened?" Nathan asked as he tried to catch his breath.

"What's the matter?" Daley asked at the same time.

"This," said Eric, holding out the metal box, which by now had taken on a potentially ominous aura. "First of all, I found it buried on the beach, up near the tree line. Second, it's mine, as are all its contents. I found it. I'm gonna keep it." He paused for maximum effect. "Finders keepers," he said, "losers weepers."

He then placed the box in the center of their circle and sat down himself.

Now they were all there staring at the box.

"This really is *Treasure Island*," Lex whispered to Taylor.

"*Treasure Island*? What're you talking about? *Lost*, maybe. Or what's that other one? The one with the really good-looking guys, where the girls are all so hot!"

Lex sighed.

"Let's pass it around, Eric, so we can all feel it," Melissa suggested.

With great hesitation, Eric got the container and started it on its rounds. Each in turn looked at it and carefully shook it a little, listening for a clue and feeling for some indication of meaning. Nathan shook it gently. Something rattled inside. But it wasn't especially heavy. He handed it on to Melissa. Finally it got back to Eric, who placed it again at their center.

"Now what?" asked Nathan. He was eager to find out what was inside.

"Oh! I know," Melissa said. "Let's all guess what's in it."

"We've pretty much done that," said Jackson.

"Then why don't we each pretend it's ours and

tell each other what we'd *like* it to be," Melissa suggested. "You know, like if we opened it, what we'd like to reach in and find."

"Oh swell, gang!" Eric said, doing his best Beaver Cleaver imitation. "That sounds like a *really* neat-o, peachy keen thing to do."

"So why not?" Daley piped up. "If it's your box, Eric, you go first."

"Is that an order, Daley?" he said.

"Oh, forget it, Eric. Your whole act is getting lame."

"All right, all right, whatever."

"So," Daley said, "what would you like to find in there if you opened it?"

Eric sighed dramatically to make sure they all understood this wasn't his sort of game, but he continued to stare at the box.

"Okay," he said slowly, easing himself into their game in spite of himself. "If I had my wishes, I'd like to have a pair of really cool sunglasses." He paused. "Then . . . a roll of toilet paper, frankly." At which point all the other kids snickered. "Then, I'd like to have a humongous chocolate bar. And last . . ." He held his hand up to his ear as if he were holding a cell phone. But then he looked embarrassed. Nathan had a hunch he was going to say he wished he had a satellite phone or some kind of massive radio so he could call his mom.

Hey, Nathan thought, *I'm with you on that one.*

"That's all," Eric said abruptly. He handed the box to Daley.

She looked at it for a minute, then said, "Toothpaste, first. And some dental floss. And, yes, Eric, some toilet paper, too. Bug spray, I think. And, um . . . ah! A huge ice-cream cone."

Then it was Melissa's turn. "I'd like to reach in there and have a furry, sweet little kitten I could pet and feed and look after and play with. And some more toilet paper, too."

"Okay," said Lex, after they passed him the box. "A book. A compass. Some more seeds. A hand mirror to signal with. And—okay—some toilet paper, too, I guess."

"For me," said Taylor, "I'd start with the toilet paper. But after that, a mirror like Lex wants, but not to signal anything. I'd be able to get my hair done right. And a nail file. And some mouthwash—for everybody! Then some shampoo and conditioner. And some deodorant!"

"Well," Nathan said, "other than the toilet paper, I think there's only one thing I'd want . . ."

In his head—from the very beginning of their little game—he knew what he wanted. He wanted a walkie-talkie, and he knew exactly why and exactly what he'd do with that little radio. He would talk to Daley. He would find her with the radio. If he had that walkie-talkie he could *communicate* with her, *speak* to her, let her know how he felt about her, do the one thing he had always been so very good at—talking! But Daley could be so remote, could keep herself at such a distance.

He looked up and saw the others looking at

him with grins and raised eyebrows.

"I'd want a walkie-talkie," he finished. He was going to say more, follow up with some blather about contacting airplanes that were looking for him. Or search parties setting out cross-country to find them and save them. But it all seemed dumb when you put it that way.

So he didn't say anything more.

"You through?" Jackson asked.

"Your turn," said Nathan.

Jackson took the box, then said, "I think there's only one thing I'd really like to have from that box, and that's a harmonica."

"A harmonica?" Melissa asked.

"Can you play one of those?" Lex asked, the reverence in his voice unmistakable.

"Mm-hm." Everybody waited expectantly for him to talk about it more. But he just gazed off into the trees.

EIGHT

"I can *not* believe this," Eric was saying. This time he wasn't even screaming. "I really cannot believe that you could vote to let a ten-year-old kid draw up plans for our shelter." He stopped long enough to take a deep breath. "He's only ten years old, guys. Ten!"

"First, it's great to hear you talk about *our* shelter," Daley said. "Keep up the good attitude. Second, I know, Lex may only be ten. But he's also the only one of us here who really understands how to do lots of things."

"Pardon *moi!*" Eric said.

"Eric," Melissa said, "we've just voted for it. This is what Lex is good at."

"Well *I* didn't vote for him."

"Beside the point, Eric," Nathan said. "The rest of us did."

Eric shrugged. "Okay," he said. "And may I assume that Queen Daley—the winner's sister—will soon be giving us her orders?"

"You better believe it," Daley snapped back.

She took a breath, collecting herself.

"Look, guys, as Lex gets further along with his plans for the shelter, we'll have more complete lists of things he'll need to build it with. Obviously there'll be bamboo, wood, twine, whatever. We'll *all* have to help find, gather, and haul the stuff down here. Then we'll *all* have to help put it together. Eric, I really don't see how else it can be done. Do you?"

Eric shrugged again.

"I mean," she went on, "how else can you *do* something besides *doing* it? *Your* little palace wasn't exactly a first-rate example of how to get it done."

Eric flushed angrily.

"All right," Daley said, "let's spend the day gathering as much food as we can. That way we'll have provisions while we work, and we won't have to run off all the time looking for food. Then we'll get together late in the afternoon. Lex should have a plan by then."

Melissa and Jackson went back to the tent to see if it had been seriously damaged when the center pole got knocked down during the confusion the previous night. Fortunately, everything was repairable. They started tightening ropes and doing other minor maintenance.

"Well," Melissa said after they had been working for a while. "We seem to be doing okay on the democracy front."

Jackson didn't say anything for a minute as he tied up the tent's side flaps to air it out.

"Daley's democracy," he said, as though he was testing to see how the words tasted. "I think it's probably a waste of time."

"Why?"

"I don't know, Melissa. I've got a hunch that when people really don't like the results of all this voting business, they'll go on and do what they want anyway. And when that happens, end of democracy."

"But we've all agreed to the principle of the thing."

"Principle." Jackson's face looked skeptical. "You can agree to anything in principle. It's when the principle runs up against what some real person thinks or wants that you get problems."

"Well, I think it'll work," she said with emphatic belief. "I mean, it's *got* to, hasn't it?" she finished with a sinking feeling that she might well be wrong.

"Melissa," Jackson answered after finishing with the tent flaps, "principles are abstract. People are real. We'll see."

N^INE

ate in the afternoon everyone finished the tasks they'd been working on—or, in the case of Eric, *not* working on—and they gathered around the fire pit to hear Lex's plan.

"A dome," Lex said. "I think the best kind of structure would be a dome. It'd be stronger than a teepee kind of thing, and it can be a lot bigger, too. A lot more cubic footage."

Lex was excited and a little nervous. In preparation for his presentation, he had gathered some slender twigs from trees around the area, sharpened them, and burned them in a fire. They did okay as pencils. Then he had drawn a rough sketch of what he was talking about on the one white shirt he still had. Then he'd cordoned off a section of the beach up near the tree line, smoothed it off as perfectly as he could, and redrawn his diagrams in the sand, large enough for all of them to see.

"What's all that stuff?" Taylor said.

"Give me a minute," Lex said.

He went to the edge of the jungle to gather up some of the much-darker earth in there, came back out, and carefully filled in the lines he had drawn in the sand. That way everybody would be able to see what he was actually talking about when he did his presentation. Everybody leaned over his diagram on the sand, straining to see what he was doing. No one seemed to get it.

"Clueless!" Taylor said finally.

"A dome," Lex said again. "A geodesic dome."

The older kids looked at him blankly.

"Geo-*what*-ic?" Eric said.

"I know, I know," Lex said. "A geodesic dome seems kind of ambitious. I mean, materials are the big challenge."

"Yeah, that was precisely my thought, too," Eric said. "Materials are the big challenge."

"Shut up, Eric," Nathan said.

Lex cleared his throat. "First I thought about bending bamboo to form the top of the shelter. But I tested it, and bamboo breaks too easily when you bend it. It would probably take high-pressure steam machines or something to do that kind of job."

The other kids looked at each other. They

seemed impressed . . . but also a little lost.

"So then I thought about cutting down some of the trees to make the shelter. But most of the trees are too big. We can't really use them unless we saw them up lengthwise, you know, make planks, and there's no way we could even begin to do that with that little saw we have.

"So if we *did* try to use whole trees, we'd have to use them log cabin–style—stack 'em on top of one another—and I don't think there are enough of us to do that much work. That's really heavy stuff, and we'd need more of a foundation and probably forms and all."

"Well, I'm glad *some*body around here's thinking about my poor back," Eric put in. "I've hauled enough water to know what *heavy* means."

Lex continued without comment. "So a geodesic dome seemed like the best solution."

He looked around and waited for comments.

"Uh . . ." Nathan said.

"Hm . . ." Daley said.

Everybody went silent.

"Okay, Lex," Taylor spoke up. "Can we back up a little? What *is* a geowhatever dome?" She looked around menacingly, ready to back up her supposition. "And I'll betcha a dollar I'm not the only one around here who doesn't know."

"Oh!" It hadn't occurred to him that nobody else would know what a geodesic dome was. "It's a dome invented by this guy named R. Buckminster

Fuller. There're all kinds of domes, I guess. A Roman arch is like a dome. That's the kind that's round at the top and has a keystone at the very top center, so all the pressure from the rest of the stones pushes in on it, and it's real strong, so it's put in last. Now, the Gothic arch—"

"Lex," said Nathan. "Stay focused, please."

Lex frowned. He realized that he needed to finish giving them the plan. It's just that architecture was so *interesting*.

"*Geodesic* domes, Lex," Melissa said softly.

"Right." He scratched his head. "I thought it might be the best to build because all the pieces you use to make it are the same size. That would cut down a lot on the time we'd have to spend, because once we got the first length of bamboo we needed, we could cut all the rest to that one piece. We wouldn't need lots of different-size pieces."

Lex stopped.

"Well?" Jackson said.

"Well what?" Lex replied.

"Lex, you've got something to show us in the sand?" Daley prompted.

"Oh. Yeah."

The group looked down at the sand drawing of what Lex envisioned the dome would look like when finished—along with various sketches of cross sections and even some computations involving dimensions and other matters. They almost didn't know what to say.

"Can I just say," Eric said, "that's genius. Total genius."

"Thank you," Lex said.

"Problem is," Eric said, "I have no idea what it means."

"Here, look." Lex had brought out three pieces of bamboo to test his theory. He'd cut them to the same length, then notched the ends and made holes.

"So, I lay these three pieces on the ground like so." He demonstrated. "Then I slide these three pins made from bamboo into these holes. Here, here, here." He picked up the result of his work: a triangle, three feet on each side. "Voilà!" he said triumphantly.

Everyone looked at the triangle and blinked.

"Great, gang!" Eric said. "We're gonna live in a three-square-foot triangle. That's super-duper, Lex."

Jackson gave him a look. Eric went quiet.

But looking around the group, Lex could tell they still didn't have the first clue what he was getting at.

"This triangle is just a building block," he said. "The whole dome is composed of this same triangle repeated over and over in a pattern that makes—"

Lex realized he'd totally forgotten the most important part of his presentation. No wonder they couldn't see what he was talking about! He ran behind a nearby bush and came out with a small-scale model he'd made. It was an accurate model of the dome he had in mind, made entirely from reeds he'd gathered in the marsh at the far end of the beach. It was composed of a series of simple triangular structures—miniature versions of the one lying on the sand. When fitted together, they made a perfect little dome.

"Ta-da!" he said, setting the tiny dome on the sand in the middle of the group.

"Oh," Eric said. "A jungle gym."

"Yes!" Lex said. "It's like a jungle gym!"

"Oh!" Suddenly everyone seemed to get it. It *did* look like one of those old jungle gyms they had played on when they were kids.

"Looks kinda flimsy, though," Eric said.

"Watch," Lex said. He picked up a half-full five-gallon jug of water. "What's this weigh? Twenty pounds?" He set it gingerly on top of the little dome. The dome made a slight creaking noise. But it didn't give way.

They all looked at one another for a moment. Then smiles broke out throughout the group. Jackson seemed to sum it up for all of them.

"Awesome, Lex!" he said.

"Ab-so-*lute*-ly!"

For once, even Eric agreed.

Daley

Now we're getting somewhere. We know

where we're building, and what we're building, and even what we're building it with. Now all I have to do is keep everyone talking to each other long enough to actually build it.

"Okay," Daley said after everyone had finished oohing and aahing at Lex's little model. "Is everybody ready to get started?"

There was a chorus of yesses. She hadn't seen everybody this enthusiastic in days. Lex's plan seemed to have gotten everyone fired up.

"Okay," Daley went on. "Let's see some hands in the sky so I can count."

All hands went up.

"Thank you," she said. "Now, the guys will have to be doing most of the heavy work—that's cutting down the bamboo, then chopping it to length, then hauling it to the site. Taylor will have to weave husks and vines into twine. Melissa, you'll braid vines and notch the ends of the bamboo pieces. I'll collect palm fronds to start making the roof and sides. And since we'll be working extra hard—and in the heat—we'll need extra water. So, Eric, that'll be your job."

"Oh, wow," Eric said. "Why am I not surprised?"

"Okay, everybody," Daley said, clapping her hands, "let's get to it."

But before anybody moved, Eric called out loudly, "Okay, hold on, everybody listen!"

Great, Daley thought. *Now we'll never get started.*

But before she could cut him off, he continued. "Some of you have maybe thought I was just being a jerk around here—and I maintain my rights to continue being one if I feel like it—but just so you'll *stay off my back* about the ammo box—and I still assert my rights to it and to its contents . . ."

He held them with a long pause.

"But the moment of truth has arrived, and"— he paused dramatically to play his little scene out as long as he could—"I will now get that box and we will open it and see what's inside."

He gestured at the box, which he had set down in a clear spot on the sand.

Daley felt a burst of irritation. Everybody had been getting all ready to go. But as soon as Eric mentioned the box, they all dropped what they were doing and surrounded it.

"Hold on!" Daley said. "Nice try, Eric. But we've got a lot of work to do yet."

Eric looked sullen.

Nathan nodded. "Good point!" he said. "We've got a *lot* of work to do yet."

"Let's start breaking ground first," Daley said. "And when we've gotten an actual start to our shelter, *then* let's go open the box."

They all groaned, but they started drifting back over toward her.

"We need to mark off the area first. We can put

stakes in the ground made from sticks."

"Bamboo," Lex said. "Bamboo would be better. I've done a very careful study of the materials available around here and—"

Daley could see he was about to go off on a big dissertation about the comparative advantages of bamboo versus wood, so she interrupted him. "Okay, so it would probably be a good idea for us all to have some *bamboo* stakes so we can actually see where the thing's gonna be. So we'll have to pass the knife around and sharpen the stakes—"

"Why not have Jackson sharpen a bunch of them?" Lex suggested. "It's his knife, after all; he made it himself, and he's probably better at carving and stuff than the rest of us."

"Good idea," Nathan put in, "then you can help explain your drawings to us so we get a better idea of what we'll be doing when we actually start working."

So Jackson whittled away at a number of spearlike sticks to mark the hard-packed ground, while Lex explained more to the rest of them.

When Jackson was through, they all took their sticks and marked off a square about thirty by thirty feet. Then, within that square, they drew a circle touching each side of the square at one point.

As they worked, they continued to speculate about what was in Eric's metal box.

"It's totally just gonna be used ammo," Nathan said.

"What if there's a map or something?" Lex said.

"What good would that do us?" Taylor said.

When they had finished making a square, they stepped off the diameter.

"We'll need a hole at the center for the central support," Lex said.

Nathan grabbed a shovel and began scooping out a hollow at the exact center.

"What if it's a radio?" Melissa said, pointing at the box.

"Radios back then were made from vacuum tubes," Lex said. "A radio with the power of a modern cell phone was the size of a backpack and weighed about fifty pounds."

Everyone continued to speculate as Nathan dug.

"There," Nathan said finally, tossing the shovel aside.

They all stood back and admired the lines in the sand and the hole Nathan had dug marking the center.

"I guess that's going to be the focus of our world for a while," Melissa said.

"I guess so," Daley agreed.

Then Nathan went to the center of the circle and jammed his pole deep into the hole, declaring, "I claim thee for our house and home!"

They all laughed, and then Eric—nearly whispering—said, "Now can I go get *my* box so we can open *my* box?"

Everybody looked expectantly at Daley.

Daley looked up at the sky. It was already late in the afternoon. They probably wouldn't get much more done. And they still needed to gather some more food before dinner time.

"Sure, Eric," she said. "Why not?"

There were cheers from the group as Eric went back alone to where he had stowed the box. When he got back, they reformed their circle with the treasure again in the center.

They all stared at it, but some still had reservations about opening it up, or about how to do it.

"Let's throw rocks at it from over there," Melissa suggested. "It could have a whatcha-macallit in it."

"A grenade?" Lex said.

"Yeah."

"No, that's no good," said Eric. "I'll just whack it with a rock right here."

"No, no, no," Daley said. "That's just what might set it off."

But before they could get into another fight, Jackson strode over to the thing, squatted, and flipped the locking snaps.

"Wait!" Melissa called.

But it was too late. Jackson had already opened

the top. And nothing happened. Nothing at all.

"There," he said. "No bomb. Eric? It's all yours now."

Everyone gathered eagerly around the box.

Eric looked cautiously inside before reaching into the box. Then he started to take things out. First, there was a pocket watch. Eric looked at it, shook it a little, then passed it on. Next, he took out a cap, a military fatigue cap, pretty much the worse for wear, but still identifiable. After that, snapshots of some young men in military clothes and combat boots. Eric looked at the pictures, then handed them around.

The photos were black and white, curling and yellowed with age. They were mainly of one man with his smiling buddies, and one of him by himself holding a rifle at a port-arms position. In another he was holding a little monkey he had apparently taken as a pet. The soldiers were all smiling, usually shirtless, crop-haired, and young—barely older than the kids there in the sand passing their photos around.

"I guess they're marines," Jackson said. "It was mostly marines out in the Pacific, I think."

"Yeah. It's got that globe-and-anchor logo." Eric pointed at the insignia on the hat. Daley recognized it as the symbol of the United States Marine Corps.

Daley was turning the watch over and over in her hand as if she was looking for an inscription. "I wonder how old it is," she mused.

"And look," said Eric, pulling out a chain that still held two metal tags.

"Those are dog tags," said Nathan.

"Is his name on them?" Lex asked.

"Let's see," Eric said. "Yes. And I guess that's his serial number. Don't they all have serial numbers?"

"Right," said Jackson. "And look, that's his blood type, then a letter *P*."

"What's that?" asked Taylor.

"I'm not sure," said Lex, "but I think it's his religion."

"What's a religion starting with P?" Taylor asked.

"Presbyterian?" Nathan suggested.

"Or probably Protestant," Lex said. "But what was his name?"

"It says WALTERS, MATTHEW D."

"Anything else?" Daley said.

"Nah," Eric said.

"Wait. Look." Lex pointed. Clinging to the side of the box was a white rectangle.

Jackson put his hand into the box. "A letter," he said, holding up a sheet of yellowed paper, threatening to fall apart. He handed it carefully to Melissa.

"Awesome," she murmured. "It's dated July 1944."

"World War II," Lex said.

"This thing has been floating around for more than sixty years," Nathan looked incredulous.

"Whoa, that's almost all the way back to Vietnam!" Taylor said.

Nathan rolled his eyes. "Uh, Taylor? World War II was like twenty years before Vietnam."

"Well, how was I supposed to know that?" she said hotly.

"It's like a time capsule," Daley said, hoping to defuse the little outburst.

"This letter," Melissa said. "It's a letter he wrote home. To his folks."

"Read it, Melissa," said Nathan.

She read it aloud to them.

"Dear Mom and Dad. I hope you haven't been worrying about me too much, but we've been pretty busy lately. This is an out-of-the-way sort of place, not like some of your bigger engagements. When we came ashore, we didn't think there were any Japanese here, but later we found out different. A lot different. We didn't have but one actual battle, but that was enough for most of us. After that, we haven't seen much of the Japanese. Word from above is that quite a few of them are still here, but I guess we'll find out about that eventually and deal with it then.

"But in the meantime we're here on this beautiful island. The guys in my unit are a great bunch. We're from all over the States. Mostly that makes

for a lot of fun. There are some Southern guys, and you wouldn't believe some of their drawls. And a bunch from New England who are a pretty quiet group until you get used to them. Some of us are sons of icemen and ditch diggers, and others are sons of doctors and lawyers. But we all manage to work together pretty darned well.

"Anyway, I hope I can write a lot more often than I have been. Try not to worry. I'm doing okay, and believe me, I'm planning to make it back home. Right now I'm living in paradise, so you've got nothing to worry about.

"I love you and I miss you both very much. Give my love to Sissy and Byron, too, and give Gramma a special big hug."

Melissa got choked up as she finished the letter.

"There's a PS," she said. But then she couldn't keep going. She was openly crying and trying to wipe her tears away. She passed the letter back to Eric, who carefully refolded it and set it down gently in the ammo box.

"Living in paradise," Daley said softly.

For a moment everyone was quiet.

"In the military, you weren't supposed to ever take those dog tags off," Nathan said finally. "If those are his dog tags, it doesn't look like he made it back."

"Neither did his letter," Melissa was finally

able to say. "Oh, his poor mother and father. Isn't there some way we could find out who they are and send this to them?"

"Melissa," said Eric. "They're probably long dead by now. Besides, uh . . ." And he simply raised his hands and looked around.

They were all quiet again until Jackson stood, gripping his bamboo pole.

"Tell you what, guys. Sixty years from now I don't want somebody reading an old letter of mine to find out what happened to us. I plan to be there and tell them myself!"

With that, he walked to the center of the circle and planted his pole next to Nathan's.

"There! That backs up *my* vote for Lex."

Then Melissa, then Lex, then Daley, then even Taylor and Eric planted their poles as well. In one last gesture, Jackson gathered up the dog tags from the sand and wrapped them around the poles with the chain that had held them dangling from the neck of Walters, Matthew D., a boy from so many years ago who, in all likelihood, had never grown old.

Daley walked to the dog tags hanging on the pole and fingered them momentarily. They were warm and smooth, barely aged after sixty years in the ammo box.

Jackson's right, she thought. *I'm not dying here, either.*

TEN

The next day everyone was up early. There was a sense of expectation in the air as they set to work. Soon Nathan and Lex were busy with the flooring for the shelter, Melissa was tending to her weaving of vines into twine, and Jackson was working the saw in the stand of bamboo.

Into this hive of activity, Eric came stumbling back carrying water from the well. When he saw he was in sight of the others, he dropped the jugs with a huge groan and fell to the ground.

"Hey, people!" he managed to call out. "Look, I'm trying to be a good member of this team. For real, I am. But there's gotta be *something* else I can do. Don't you understand how *heavy* water is? Don't you remember when the plane crashed how hard we hit? I think I may have cracked a vertebra or something. Seriously, my back is not gonna last much longer."

"Suits me, Eric," Nathan answered without stopping his work. "How are your lashing skills?"

"What do you mean, 'lashing'?" he asked.

"Forget it," Nathan said. "I don't have time to waste explaining it to you."

Eric scowled. Nathan, always with his superior attitude. Nobody understood how seriously injured his back was. Well, it *might* be injured, anyway. It sure was sore. What if he *did* have a cracked vertebra? He might wake up tomorrow and find he'd suddenly been paralyzed from the waist down.

Lex walked over and looked down at Eric.

"Here, I'll help," he said. He tried to lift the heavy jugs, but they were clearly too heavy for him. "I think I can, I think I can, I think I can," he chanted, moving only a few inches at a time and staggering comically. Lex was doing a pretty good performance, making a big joke out of how hard it was. "Oh, my back! Oooh, my back!"

"Very funny, Lex. You're a real comedian." Eric grabbed the two jugs, set them down at the edge of the site, then picked up two more empties and trudged back to the well.

Lex and Nathan giggled as Eric walked away.

"I heard that!" he called.

Melissa was coming toward him down the trail, her arms full of vines. Eric stumbled slightly and groaned, hoping to get some sympathy from her.

"Melissa, please," he panted. "This is killing me. Can't we swap jobs?"

"Sure," she said. "You good at braiding rope?"

Braiding rope. With all the blisters on his hands from working on his house the other day, that sounded even worse than carrying water. At least with the water he could go out and fool around near the well without a bunch of accusatory eyes pointing out everything he was doing wrong.

Groaning a second time, he staggered on, getting into the performance so much that he almost forgot the jugs were empty. Still on the lookout for someone else who might be willing to trade jobs with him, he saw Daley coming his way, her arms loaded with dirty laundry. Not an easy touch, he thought—but anything seemed better than what he was doing. Putting on a jaunty air and a happy smile, he said, "Last chance for you to get the water for a while, Daley."

"Okay," she said. "Here's the laundry, but there'll probably be more in a while." She gave him an evil smile. "Very stinky. Lots of scrubbing in hot, soapy water."

Eric actually thought about it for two seconds. *Hot* water? *Soapy* water? Lots of scrubbing? That would *kill* his poor hands. His smile faded.

"Never mind," he said.

Then he plodded ahead, feeling sorrier and

sorrier for himself. Off just a short way he saw Jackson taking a breather from his sawing. It crossed his mind to offer to swap with him, too. But just the thought of touching a saw made his hands burn.

Last of all he spotted Taylor at the tent. She was brushing her hair.

Last chance, dude, he thought.

"Taylor," he almost barked at her. "You're not making any rope. You're not weaving any vines. You're not cutting down any trees. You're not doing anything useful. Would you *pleeease* lug some water?" Then, as an afterthought, "Would you please *help* me lug some water? You won't have to do it all yourself. I promise."

Taylor stopped brushing and simply stared at him. Then she broke out into a deep, throaty laugh.

"Omigod!" She snorted. "For a second there you had me, Eric. I almost thought you were serious!" Still laughing, she turned back into the tent.

Eric just stared after her, his sense of fairness finally crumbling. "That's it," he fumed to himself. "I've had it! I quit! I am *done!*"

And with that, Eric threw the jugs down and turned to go back to the fire pit.

Inside the tent, Taylor was only vaguely aware that Eric had gone—presumably to get more water. But she had other things on her mind, namely a growing concern about her complexion. This sun, she thought, this salt air, she considered, this damp and heat, she fretted, were all very bad for her skin. At home, of course, someone who was going to be a model, and, like, an actress, even, was able to take proper care of things like that. But out here in this, like . . . like . . . like, well, jungle, who could take care of themselves? What if she got back and had crow's-feet around her eyes! She'd look like an old lady! Everyone would laugh!

And her future would be wrecked!

Suddenly her skin seemed to be shrinking up, cracking, wrinkling, burning—squeezing her entire body and sucking the very saliva out of her mouth. She tried to swallow, but nothing much happened. Her throat was terribly dry, like she was on a desert island with a mouth full of sand instead of a jungle island with a mouth full of . . . whatever. She felt that if she could move her head and actually look at her skin she would see it all raised up in what one of her mother's aunts always used to call chisel bumps—goose bumps.

She looked into the mirror and saw . . .

A lizard.

Oh God! It had happened. She'd changed into a lizard.

And then she thought, *Wait a minute! There's no mirror here.*

Which meant . . .

She was *really* looking at a lizard. A *huge* lizard. Four feet long, green, with speckles and a long, slithery tail. The lizard stared back at her with huge yellow eyes.

Scream! she thought.

But nothing came.

Scream, her head said. *No way*, her throat seemed to say back. *Please try*, her head said again. *Okay*, her throat said, *but don't expect any miracles here*, and it squeezed out a great big squeak.

Nathan had been keeping an eagle eye on Daley, waiting for a moment when they would be alone. With them all working together on the shelter, he was beginning to think it would never happen. But suddenly he noticed everybody was gone from the little clearing. Everybody but him and Daley.

"Daley," he called as he approached. "Listen, I really need to talk to you about something."

"Well, let's walk as we talk." She had made two stacks of bamboo, one set of finished struts and one that still needed the holes drilled in the ends. "There's lots to do."

"Hold on, hold on," Nathan said.

She stopped, brushing back a strand of auburn hair, and looked at him questioningly.

Nathan could feel his pulse racing. "Yeah, well, I know there's lots to do, Daley, but I wanted to talk to you—you know, in private. Sorta."

"Private," she repeated.

Nathan looked around. They were still alone. *Okay*, he thought. *Now or never!* "Well," he said, "you know we've always been pretty . . . competitive."

"That's putting it kind of mildly, Nathan."

"I guess so." Nathan smiled weakly. "But, the thing is, I'd like to drop all that. We've been at it since we were three or whatever, and I'd like to be more, well, friends."

She squinted at him. "No more competition— that's what you're saying?"

"Exactly."

She shrugged. "Sounds good to me."

"But, well, I mean—"

Suddenly there was an odd squeak from the tent.

They both stopped and looked toward the general direction of the sound, but nothing else happened, so Nathan tried to get the conversation back on track.

"But not just noncombatants, see . . ." He broke off, tongue-tied. *God! Can't I just say it?*

Daley leaned forward, looking vaguely confused. "What?"

"I mean, if we . . ." He cleared his throat. "You and me . . ."

There was another noise from the tent. This time it was a full-on scream.

Daley's head jerked toward the tent.

"That's Taylor!" Daley said. "What in the world . . ."

And they both started to run toward the tent.

They got there just in time to see Taylor exit the tent, a hand over her heart, her eyes wild with fear.

"A dinosaur," she yelled. "Godzilla," she screamed. "It's in the tent. It's in my stuff! It was staring at me like it was taking my measurements."

"You're sure it's not a *Glamour* photographer who followed us here just to spy on you?" Daley snickered.

"Seriously, Taylor," Nathan said. "What are you talking about?

"Oough," she replied, spreading her hands as far apart as she could. "Oough," was all she could say again.

"What?"

"Lizard!" she screamed.

Nathan rolled his eyes. Some cute little gecko or chameleon had probably crawled inside the tent, and now Taylor was flipping out, making a big scene, scamming herself a little attention. He went inside the tent with a sigh.

He looked around for just a second before he saw the lizard.

Okay! he thought. *Not a gecko.*

It was huge.

He froze. The monstrous lizard stared at him. Then its tongue flicked out, making a sound like sandpaper on concrete. Nathan decided if he didn't move, maybe it would ignore him.

It started to lumber toward him. Nathan evacuated the tent at least as fast as Taylor had.

"It *is* Godzilla," he said, clearing his throat slightly. "Not quite as big as Taylor made out, but big enough. Maybe four feet long?"

"What's it doing?" Daley asked.

"Doing? Well, it's not exactly *doing* anything. It's just kinda *there*. You know. Flicking out its tongue and everything."

"It's *Jurassic Park* in there, Daley," Taylor said. "It tried to kill me. The thing's a monster!"

"Seriously, do you think it's dangerous, Nathan?" Daley asked.

"I don't have a clue," Nathan said. "Where's Lex? He knows about things like that."

"I don't know exactly," Daley said. "I think he and Jackson went to the garden to see how it was doing."

"Oh, great!" Taylor said. "He's out playing with Jackson when I've got one of those kimono lizards rifling through my knapsack. I saw on TV, they eat people and everything!"

"It is not a *Komodo* dragon," Nathan said as coolly as he could.

Just then, Lex, Jackson, and Melissa came up at a trot.

"There a lizard in the tent?" Jackson asked.

"Yeah," Daley answered, "but we don't know if it's poisonous or not."

"Usually not," Lex said. "Well, probably not, but some of them can bite a little. Lots of nasty bacteria in their teeth, though. It could cause an infection, which could lead to blood poisoning, necrosis, gangrene—"

Nathan looked at Lex. "Okay, okay, we get the point."

Everybody took turns peeking into the tent.

"What are we gonna do?" Melissa said.

Nathan was feeling let down because he hadn't been able to have his conversation with Daley. But this might be an opportunity to make himself look good in front of her. Which was better than nothing.

"Tell you what," he said. "Let me handle it."

Taylor wouldn't come within ten feet of the tent, and Eric was over near the fire pit, but Melissa and Jackson looked ready to help as best as they could.

"Um, any thoughts, Jackson?" Nathan cleared his throat and peeped in again. The lizard had not gotten any smaller. Truth was, the thing gave him the willies. Now that he'd said he was going to do it, he was wishing he'd kept his mouth shut. "I mean, I could just go in there and jab it with a stick or something. But I'd hate to, uh, hurt the wildlife, you know?"

"If we opened up the front flap," Jackson said, "it might just come on out by itself. It's probably as scared as we are."

"I mean, I'm not *scared*," Nathan said.

A tiny smile came and went on Jackson's face. "Okay, hey, take it away, bro." Jackson gestured at the tent with his hand, like, *You first.*

Nathan slowly, cautiously eased up to the front flap, but when the lizard leaped hard against the inner wall of the tent, Nathan jumped just as hard away from it. "Whoa!" he shouted.

"Any other ideas?" Jackson asked.

"He's scared," Melissa said.

"Who?" Jackson said. "Nathan? Or the lizard?"

"Ha ha," Nathan said.

The lizard thumped against the tent wall and Nathan leaped backward again.

"Okay, okay, maybe a little," Nathan said.

"Lures," Lex said. "Do you think we can lure him out?"

"Let's get some fruit and make a trail away from the tent. Toward the jungle," Nathan said.

"Do lizards like fruit?" Melissa asked.

Everybody looked at Lex. Lex shrugged.

"I'll go scrounge up some fruit if you want," Jackson said.

He started away, but stopped and turned back to them.

"But what if we'd just be luring some more lizards *this* way? Into the tent?"

"Oooh!" Taylor shouted.

After he'd announced to himself that he was quitting the water-carrying chore, Eric went back to the fire pit. He was fuming at the various outrages that had been inflicted upon him, but he wanted to convince the rest of the crew that he had just cause to complain. So he began rehearsing the possibilities.

"It's over. I'm done!" *That's pretty strong,* he thought.

"C'mon, guys. It's not fair." *Nah, too whiny.*

"I've carried more water than anyone, and that's a fact." *Pretty logical.*

"This is the most important job here. Do you really want to trust a guy like me with it?" *They'd probably go for that one.*

"I might really mess this up. With all the boiling and filtering and—"

Whoa, he thought. *Boiling.*

Eric looked around at the community stuff kept near the fire pit—the tools and stuff—and saw the ammo box. Jackson stored his lighter in one of the waterproof bins so that everyone had access to it. Eric opened it up, and there it was. The lighter.

He smiled.

Jackson had been gone for just a few minutes and came back with some reddish orange fruit that they were calling papaya—though they weren't totally sure if it was. He handed it to Nathan, who started laying a trail toward the jungle, when it occurred to Nathan that lizards probably liked insects better. But he finished his fruit trail just in case, and went back to sit with Melissa and Jackson.

"I guess this could take a while," Nathan finally said.

"Well, we can take turns watching if you want."

"Nah. I'll stay here, too," Jackson said.

After some time, Melissa went off for a minute and came back with a longish stick.

"I'm going to try to get that flap open again."

She crept up to the tent, stretched herself as far as she could, and hooked the stick on a corner of the flap. She'd started to ease it back when the lizard leaped at the stick, grabbed it, and shook it.

Melissa raced back to Nathan.

"Well," she muttered. "So much for that."

Eric had a plan. This whole water thing was getting to be a serious hassle. What if it caused him to develop some kind of serious back problem? Maybe he didn't actually have a cracked vertebra . . . but what if he developed a slipped disk or something? That would be disastrous. Not just for him, but for everybody.

Nah, he needed a break.

He looked around quickly. He'd already accomplished half the plan. There was just one minor thing to take care of. He was alone at the new fire ring they'd built in the clearing where they were going to build the shelter. He just needed to make sure nobody saw him.

Then he heard something, so he looked up and saw Daley, Lex, and Taylor coming toward him. He didn't want to explain why he had the lighter, so he stuck it under the pile of laundry Daley had dumped there earlier. Spotting two empty jugs nearby, Eric picked them up as if he was going on another water run.

"Hey!" he called to the group as they got closer. "What was all the screaming and yelling about?"

"A lizard got into the tent," Lex said.

Taylor flounced past Eric and flopped down next to the fire pit.

"I hate this place," she said. "I really do."

Daley picked up one of the full jugs of water and poured it into the nose cone from the plane. They had been using the cone to boil water. She carried the cone to the ring of stones where the fire was.

"That's no lizard. It's a sci-fi film that shouldn't have been made," Taylor grumbled.

"The others are trying to coax it out now, but—what the—" Daley stared at the ring. Odd. "The fire's gone out."

"Omigosh," said Eric. "I wonder how that happened?"

Daley looked hard at Eric as she went to the storage bin.

"It just stared at me," Taylor was explaining. "It looked like it was measuring me up and down for a meal."

Daley opened the bin and frowned. "Where's the lighter?" Daley asked.

"Should be in the bin, Daley," Lex said.

"Should be, but it's not."

"Well, where else would it be?"

"Good question, Lex," Eric said. "Well, if there's no lighter, there's no fire. And I guess if there's no fire, there's no use in my going after more water. Is there?"

And with that, he dropped the two jugs to the ground, turned, and sat down near Taylor, arms behind his head as if there were no problems within a million miles of him.

Daley looked at him, then at Lex, who shrugged his shoulders. She looked back at Eric.

"Errr-iiic," she said.

He didn't turn to her.

"If you can't bring yourself to look at me," she said, "then you sure better listen to me—real hard—because if you've done something with that lighter just so you don't have to haul water, you will be sorry. You will be very, *very* sorry."

Then she knelt next to the ashes, placed her hand on them, and stood again.

"They're wet," she said, her voice quivering. "The ashes are wet. Somebody *put* the fire out."

Oh, great, Eric thought. *Here we go again. Daley's gonna flip out and go ninja on us.*

"But why would somebody want to put out the fire?" Lex asked.

"Oh, I don't know," Daley replied tensely. "Maybe because if there's no more fire, then there's no more boiling water. And if there's no more boiling water, there's no need to haul more water up from the well. Is there, Eric?"

In her speech, Daley's voice had gotten harder and harder, until at the end she was nearly yelling at Eric.

"Far-fetched, Daley," Eric looked up at the sky. "Totally far-fetched. Who could possibly do a thing like that?"

All of them stared at Eric.

"What's everybody looking at *me* for?"

"Where's the lighter, Eric?"

"Whoa. Do you really think I'd stoop to such a low trick—and just to get out of a brutal, menial, thankless job that nobody else around here will do?"

But they all continued to stare at him.

"Empty your pockets," Daley said, her voice hard.

Eric jumped to his feet.

"Okay, Madam Bullwhip. There!" He pulled out both pockets clearly showing there was nothing in them. "Now maybe you should apologize! You ought to be ashamed."

"Where did you put it?" Daley asked, unfazed by Eric's outburst.

But the scene was interrupted when Taylor jumped up.

"Is it gone?" she asked.

The others looked up and saw that Nathan was suddenly among them.

"No," he answered. "We tried to lure it out with some fruit, but it didn't seem to be working." He looked curiously at the ring of stones. "What happened to the fire?"

"Eric put it out and hid the lighter," Daley answered.

"You don't know that, Daley!" Eric shouted. "You don't know that."

"But why?" Nathan asked Daley, then turning to Eric. "Why, Eric?"

Daley stooped and gathered the dirty clothes from the ground. "To get out of fetching water," she said. "No fire, no boil, no need to fetch."

Eric started fidgeting, his eyes staring at the clothes in Daley's arms. Okay, this was going to work out fine. Daley would find the lighter in the clothes, assume someone had dropped it there by mistake, and no one would be the wiser. It'd take a while for them to relight the fire. Meantime, he'd be relaxing.

"Listen, guys. The lighter's probably just been lost a little while. You know, like, how long can it have been? It's just been misplaced somewhere. I expect it'll show up just anytime."

"You're probably right," Nathan said. "But that's no reason to shirk your work." He made a big show of picking up the camp shovel, and then started banging stakes into the ground around the circle to mark the perimeter of the dome. He put a serious expression on his face. Joe Workaholic.

If you think you're gonna shame me into working, Eric thought, *then think again, bro.*

Daley gathered up all the clothes again and dumped them into the water in the nose cone.

Uh-oh! Eric thought. He tried not to look at the clothes. Maybe the lighter would float to the top.

Daley pushed the clothes around with a stick they used for stirring the clothes when they were boiling. But since there wasn't any heat, her task was pretty pointless. Like Nathan, she seemed to enjoy showing how hard she was working while Eric did nothing.

Eric sneaked a glance at the clothes she was brutalizing. *Not good. Totally not good.* Would it destroy the lighter, being underwater? Maybe there was some way he could put this on her. If it would just float to the top, he could scoop it up and look like the hero—while accusing her of being careless. That would be excellent. It's just if the lighter *didn't* float up . . .

Daley poked viciously at the clothes with her pointy stick. "No hot water, no clean clothes." Stab. "Is this what you want, Eric?" Stab. Stab.

"Filthy clothes forever?" Stab. Stab. Stab.

Eric swallowed. How long before she impaled the lighter?

She continued jabbing at the clothes in the nose cone. "Eric, this is truly stupid. Just tell us where the lighter is."

Finally he couldn't stand it any longer. Eric rushed over and dumped the nose cone over so the water and clothes spilled out in a wet heap on the ground. Frantically, he rummaged through the wet pile.

"What are you doing?" Lex shouted.

"Just checking. Just checking," he mumbled. "It could have fallen into the dirty clothes pile."

Nothing.

Weird. Where'd it go? He stopped, looked around. Everybody was staring at him. The clothes were now a scattered, sandy mess on the ground.

"What is *wrong* with you?" Daley said.

This was bad. They were really going to be in trouble if they lost that lighter. Eric's shoulders slumped. The only sound was Nathan pounding on his stakes with the back of the shovel, the clanging of the metal on the wood . . .

. . . until one blow was followed by an unfamiliar *crunch!*

"What was that, Nathan?" Lex asked.

"I dunno," Nathan replied. Then he pounded a few more times, each with the same peculiar crunching sound.

"Sounds like a shell or something, doesn't it?"

"Oh my God," Eric said. "No, Nathan. Stop! Stop pounding!" And with that he dived at Nathan's feet and started digging madly with his hands. Finally, he saw it: splintered plastic. He pulled it out and cupped it in his hands in horror.

"What's with him?" Taylor asked. "Eric, you are weird!"

He sat up slowly, still clutching the splintered object to his chest.

"What?" Lex said. "What did you find?"

"Uh . . ." he said.

There was a long silence.

"Eric," Daley hissed.

"It's the lighter," he whispered. "I found the lighter."

They were all silent, overcome by what they had just seen, the lighter crushed and mangled beyond any possible repair.

"Oh boy," said Lex softly. "I sure hope there's somebody here who can start a fire."

ELEVEN

"I didn't know." Nathan said. "I had no idea it was in the hole."

"Gee. How did it get down there?" Eric said, his voice trembling.

"Well, let's see, Eric," Daley said. "I'll give you my best guess. How's that? I'll bet that you hid it in the laundry, because you tipped it over and started going through it. But I'll bet it fell out when I picked up the laundry and put it all in the nose cone, because that's when you got all squirrelly."

"Now wait a sec. Hold on a minute," Eric began, but he knew he couldn't bluff this one away. His voice cracked. "It . . . it wasn't supposed to happen like this. It wasn't supposed to happen at all. I wasn't trying to get rid of the lighter! Come on! I didn't mean for any of this to happen."

"But it did, Eric. Without that lighter, there's no fire," Nathan said.

"And that means no cooked food and no clean water," Lex added.

Taylor stood up, looked around at no one in particular, and said, "Have I ever told any of you how much I hate this place?" and stormed off as Eric let the smashed lighter fall to the sand.

Back at the tent, Melissa peered cautiously through a screen window in the back. She was so focused on being totally quiet, trying to see the lizard without its seeing her, that she never heard Taylor come up behind her.

"Hey," Taylor said.

Melissa jumped. "God, Taylor, don't sneak up on me like that! You scared me to death."

"Is that dinosaur gone yet?"

"Well, there may be a little problem. Maybe."

"Really? Gee, I'd never have guessed."

"I don't think it's a he. I think it's a she. I also think she's making a nest."

Taylor just stared at Melissa, her face frozen. "You mean, like, to lay eggs in? For little baby dinosaurs?"

Melissa nodded.

Taylor peered through the screen.

"In my sleeping bag, of course. Talk about your fatal attractions. Yuck!"

And she walked away muttering aloud but mainly to herself. "Can this day get *any* worse? Probably!"

Taylor meandered down to the edge of the beach and sat down—the same place she'd been hanging out when she was so depressed. She saw Jackson in the surf, fishing with the net they'd made. For some reason, just seeing him working away made her feel better. The fact that he didn't look at all bad with his shirt off was one thing. But it was more than that . . .

He worked in a steady, slow rhythm, casting, pulling it in, casting again. She stood looking at him for a long time, but he didn't seem to notice her presence. She got closer, let the waves wash over her feet. He still didn't acknowledge her.

"This is all my parents' fault," she said loudly.

Jackson looked over at her but said nothing, keeping his eyes peeled for any motion in his nets that would tell him he'd caught some supper for the group.

She sighed loudly, kicked the sand, and tossed her hair, trying to get his attention.

Finally he said, "*This* meaning what, exactly?" he asked.

"They went on a vacation, Jackson. A ski vacation? Switzerland. I could have gone with them, but they talked me into going to Palau. Now that I think about it, they didn't convince me of anything. They just said that's the way it was going to be. They insisted."

Taylor stopped a minute, as if she was just now understanding something.

"It was like they didn't want me on their trip," she went on, but stopped again.

"Hard to believe they wouldn't want you raining on their parade, Taylor."

"What do you mean by that? What kind of crack is that?"

Jackson kept his eyes on his nets, looking for signs.

"Well," he said softly, "you do demand attention. I think sometimes parents just get tired of us, and want time by themselves without, well, without us around."

Taylor got to her feet at that, getting back into one of her dreams.

"Look, I could be sitting in front of a romantic fire right now, looking at the Alps, sipping hot chocolate with some hot guy named Lars or Pierre or Frederico. But *nooo*. Here I am living in a tent that stinks just barely less than Eric's disgusting feet, with six other people and a lizard that wants to raise a family in my sleeping bag. I am tired of coconuts. I can't look another fish in its fins. My clothes are ruined and they chafe like crazy. I've never gone more than two weeks without getting highlights or two *days* without shaving my legs. I want caffeine. I want a new magazine. I want bubble gum and chocolate. I want to be back at home where all my friends are." She paused. "I want *toilet paper*!"

Jackson pulled the net in and tossed it out again.

"Is that too much, Jackson?"

He said nothing.

"Is it?"

He still said nothing.

"I want an answer, Jackson," she said, feeling as if she was about to lose it again.

Still without looking at her directly, he said, "Taylor, I think your parents love you."

She flopped back down to the sand. Then she realized how heavy her breathing was. She waited a few minutes in silence.

"Well," she said at last. "Is that really too much to ask?"

Jackson laughed.

"You think I'm a real hoot."

Jackson smirked. "Yeah, sorta."

"Well, good. Fine. I'm glad somebody's getting something out of it." At that she felt totally spent.

"Taylor, you know what I'm going to remember most, years and years from now when I think back on all this?"

She simply looked at him for his answer.

"I'm gonna remember that when things got really bad, you always made me laugh."

"Hmmph," was all she said. But she had to turn away so he wouldn't see the smile that flashed on her face.

"Well," she said, when she had finally managed to stifle the unwanted smile, "let's just hope that we're not here years and years from now. Thanks, Jackson. Thanks for letting me blow it all out."

He threw his net on the sand, then reached down to help her get up.

"Those fish will just have to catch themselves for a while," he said. Then, "Taylor, do me a favor, will you? Keep making me laugh."

It was the first time she had ever looked at him and actually *seen* him. And she liked what she saw.

"Okay, so it was stupid. But I didn't mean for the lighter to get whacked."

They were all assembled at the fire pit, the useless remains of their last fire lying there, taunting them. Daley was mad. But beyond that, she was worried. If they didn't handle this right . . . well, who knew where it might lead? People stealing stuff, hoarding stuff, cheating each other . . .

"But that doesn't make it any better, Eric," Nathan said. "That doesn't get us our fire back."

Everybody was fixating on the fire and the lighter. But there was a bigger issue, and Daley felt like they needed to get it out on the table. Right now. "Eric, there's a real problem here," Daley said.

"Like no fire, no water," Lex interrupted.

"And no tent, either," Taylor said, walking up

from the beach. "We've got a monster playing house in there, too, let's not forget. In *my* sleeping bag."

"I'm talking about something bigger, folks," Daley said.

"Bigger than the drinking water?" Melissa asked.

"Eric did something wrong," Daley started to say, but she wanted to make sure everyone understood she was on a different level at this point. "Eric did something very seriously wrong. I understand he didn't *mean* to, but is that excuse going to be enough? I'm talking about our survival here. We don't have any doctors. We don't have any antibiotics. We're hanging on the edge. There's no room for screwups."

"Oh, come on, Daley!" Eric said, looking desperately for a friendly face in the group. Daley was glad to see that everybody glared back at him, stone-faced.

"Eric," Daley went on, speaking directly to him. "We can't start that fire without the lighter. We tried. Remember?"

"Have you got a point, Daley?" Jackson asked.

"I sure do, Jackson. Oh, you can call it whatever you want—breaking the rules, being negligent or selfish or whatever. But we rely on each other for our lives. When something like this puts the entire group at risk, I think we need to come up with a better way to deal."

"Spare me the exaggeration, Daley," Eric said. "Puleeeze!" Eric had tried apologies and wheedling; now he was turning to sarcasm.

"Daley," Melissa began, "what do you mean by 'deal'?"

"We had a trial when Lex took the videotapes," Nathan reminded them. Daley glanced at Nathan, glad to have him backing her up.

"But this isn't about guilty or innocent," Daley said. "We know what happened here. It's about keeping people from doing something wrong to start with. We don't have a government. We don't have any police or teachers or parents or anybody else in authority. We've got to deal with this ourselves."

"What are you looking for, Daley? You want us to make a bunch of laws or something?" Jackson asked.

"What do you think Eric *ought* to do, Daley?" said Nathan.

"Well, he could start by admitting what a *stupid* thing it was to do. And he could admit that he understands what a *dangerous* thing it was to do. And he could be honest and strong enough to admit that he did it just to get out of work, so that made it a *lazy* thing to do, and he could admit that he doesn't think he owes anybody around here anything. But all he ever says is he didn't *mean* to get the lighter torn up. He didn't *mean* for any of it to happen. He didn't *mean* for it to end this way. So, Jackson, sorry, but for me, *didn't mean to* just won't cut it."

There was a short silence while the kids tried to organize their own thoughts.

"So basically you're talking punishment?" Jackson said.

"Punishment!" Eric screamed. "This is crazy!"

Daley ignored him. "I guess that is what I mean, 'cause the question I have is, how else do we get people to think twice before they do something that can hurt all of us? I'm really not trying to move all this into a morals thing. I'm just talking about taking responsibility. When people don't have the character to take responsibility for things on their own—" She looked Eric in the eye.

"Hey!"

"—then they have to pay the piper for what they do."

"But, Daley," Melissa said, clearly pained by the whole business, "shouldn't all that be automatic? You know, doing the right thing?"

Daley bent down and picked up the smashed and useless lighter. "Yeah, you'd think so, wouldn't you?"

"But it was an accident!" Eric pleaded.

"There you go again, Eric!" Daley threw up her hands. "You deliberately took the lighter. You deliberately hid it from us, and because of those deliberate actions of yours"—she gestured at the drowned fire pit—"we have no fire."

For the first time Nathan started looking nervous. "This," he tried to say, then had to clear his throat. "This is getting a little spooky. Making laws? I dunno."

"And doling out punishment," Jackson reminded them all.

Daley would not let herself be put down, though.

"Making laws? Yes. Doling out punishment? Yes. But, guys, we're having to build a society here, too. None of us asked to be here like this. It *is* scary. But here we are. Look out to sea. Have any of you spotted any ships out there with RESCUE MISSION written on the side, steaming toward us? We're the ones who have to figure out how to conduct ourselves as a group. Like it or not, we aren't just a bunch of kids out on a nice little holiday playing at bio-camping. We've got to figure out how to deal with this kind of stuff when it happens. What's the alternative? Jungle law? Survival of the fittest?"

Melissa finally broke the somber silence by asking, "We agreed to vote on issues. Does this count?"

"To me it pretty clearly does," Daley said.

"So if we all agree that somebody did something wrong, what do we do about it?" asked Nathan.

"That's hard, Nathan, but as I just said, we've all got to be responsible for our own actions. If there isn't some kind of punishment, what's going to stop people from doing whatever they want, no matter who gets hurt by it?"

"People," Eric broke in. "You're trying to make me into some kind of ax murderer or something. All I did was hide a lighter."

"*The* lighter, Eric," Nathan corrected. "*And* you killed the fire. On purpose."

"I think we've heard enough," Jackson said. "Let's vote. Who thinks Eric should be punished for what he did?"

This was not an easy thing to decide. No one wanted to be first, but all of them understood that something had to be done. They had to act on their own behalf.

"Okay, okay," Eric said. "A joke's a joke, and this one's gone far enough."

Daley raised her hand. Then Nathan, then Lex and Melissa, and finally the most reluctant voter of all, Taylor.

"You too?" Eric asked, unbelieving.

"We don't have a fire, Eric," she replied. "That's your fault."

"Does it have to be unanimous?" Melissa asked.

Everybody looked at Jackson, the one person who hadn't moved yet. He sat with his arms crossed.

"Let's not make a bigger deal out of this than it is," Jackson suggested.

"But it *is* a big deal, Jackson," Daley countered. "Even if you didn't vote."

"Okay. Let's think up something Eric can do

to make up for what he's done," Jackson agreed, ignoring Daley's observation. "But let's remember one thing while we do that: Eventually the lighter would have run out of fluid and flints, and we'd be right here again in the same pickle, and it wouldn't be anybody's *fault*."

"Yeah," Eric quickly put in. "Keep that in mind."

"But don't forget that we could have kept the fire going. Eric drowned it—on purpose!" Daley prodded.

"And a storm like this last one, Daley? Do you really think it wouldn't have drowned the fire, too?" Jackson persisted.

"It's the principle. If we stick together, we've got a chance here. But if we sabotage one another and undercut one another, we're gonna end up like good old Private Matthew D. Walters." She pointed at the dog tags of the vanished soldier, hanging on the pole where they were going to build their shelter. "I don't know about you, but I don't want somebody wandering onto this beach in fifty years, finding a necklace with my name engraved on it and going, 'Gosh, wonder who that poor girl was?' " She jingled the thin gold chain that hung around her neck.

"Look, if I could make a fire, I would," Eric said. "But I can't. What are you going to do, take time away from building the shelter to make a jungle jail for *me*?" He looked sourly at Lex. "You want another little building project, junior? How about you design a jail to stick me in?"

The group was quiet for a while. Daley knew she wanted Eric punished. But she hadn't thought the problem out enough to figure out what his punishment should amount to.

Finally Melissa broke their silence.

"How about this," she said. "Right now we don't have anywhere to sleep. How about Eric has to figure out a way to get the lizard out of the tent? It might not be as big a deal as making a fire, but it's going to be a real problem when the sun goes down."

Daley looked around to see how that was floating.

"Everybody okay with that?" Melissa said.

They all nodded silently.

"Let's just get this over with," Jackson said.

Well, Eric thought, *coulda gone worse.* Miss Moral Perfection could probably have conned everybody into inflicting something a lot worse on him. Like . . . *work.*

"Let's do it," he said.

He hopped up and walked toward the tent, the others trooping along behind him. A lizard, right? How bad could that be?

When they reached the tent, he stopped. The others gathered around the entrance in a semicircle.

Eric took a deep breath, let it out, squared his shoulders, and entered the tent.

Jackson sidled over close to Daley. "What if he gets hurt?" he asked in a low voice. "How does that fit into your social scheme?"

Daley knew Jackson was manipulating her, but she wasn't totally unwilling to have him do it. Certainly in her head, but also in her heart, she knew she was right about this business. Eric had to see that there were consequences when he jerked everybody around. She knew that their survival was on the line. But in spite of that, she was second-guessing herself, and *that* was scary. Very scary.

As Eric headed into the tent, she had a terrible thought. What if the lizard really was poisonous? What if he got bit and got gangrene or necrosis or some of that other stuff Lex had talked about? She felt uncertain—which was confusing. Most of the time she was certain about everything.

"Okay, Eric!" she called. "Bad idea . . . maybe."

But Eric had already gone inside the tent.

Daley walked toward the tent, but Melissa blocked her, grabbing her arm. "Leave it," she said, her voice strong and sure, her eyes holding Daley's. "Let him do the job. He's agreed to do it and the worst thing you could do right now is to stop him."

Daley stood still. Melissa seemed unusually sure of herself.

"Yeah," Daley said. "You're probably right."

Eric blinked. *Whoa!*

They weren't joking. That was one serious lizard. He stood motionless for a minute. Then he grinned.

There was a trick to dealing with reptiles. Bottom line, the things were dumb as bricks. If they could see you, they were all over you. But once they couldn't see you? They forgot you existed.

The lizard stared at Eric. Eric stared at the lizard. The lizard's tongue flicked out. Eric stuck his tongue out at the lizard. The lizard crouched slightly, as if it was getting ready to charge at him.

Okay, time to get busy.

As Eric scanned the tent, he saw a T-shirt lying on the floor. He scooped it up and waggled it in front of the lizard. The lizard jumped at it.

Eric dropped the T-shirt over the lizard's head, covering its eyes. The lizard froze.

Eric leaped on top of the lizard, binding the T-shirt over its head. The lizard's tail jerked frantically for a moment, then stopped. Eric could feel its scaly sides against his ribs as he lay on the floor of the tent.

Cool, he thought. *Nothing to it.*

Outside the tent everybody stood frozen, waiting.

Eric had been gone for probably ten seconds. But to Nathan it felt longer. What was he doing in there?

There was a brief noise, a scrabbling sound. Then silence.

Nathan looked at Daley. Her face was pale, her freckles standing out in high relief. "He'll be okay," Nathan wanted to say. But he didn't want to break the silence.

Suddenly there was a loud noise inside the tent, like something getting knocked over. Then Eric's voice, a shrill sound, "Ahhh!"

"Omigod!" Taylor said.

More thumping. The big lizard's tail lashed at the tent.

"No!" Eric shouted. "Let go of me!"

"We better do something!" Nathan said.

"I'm not going in there!" Taylor shrieked.

There was more thumping and banging. Eric grunted in what sounded like pain. It seemed like a terrible struggle was going on inside the tent.

Daley put her face in her hands. "Stupid, stupid!" she said. "How could I have done this to him?"

Jackson looked frantically. "Where's my stick?"

he asked. He was looking for the spear-shaped stick that he had carried for the first week or so on the island.

The stick was nowhere to be seen.

"Your knife!" Nathan said.

Jackson drew his knife and swallowed.

"I'll go get the medical kit!" Lex shouted. "Where is it?"

"It's in the tent!" Daley said.

Jackson was still looking at the tent, his knife out.

"Go!" Nathan said. "Or give it to me and I'll go!"

"We'll go together," Jackson said grimly.

There was another howl of pain from the tent, along with fresh banging and thumping.

Nathan looked around, saw the shovel, and grabbed it. "Let's go!" he said.

As Nathan and Jackson nervously approached the tent, the noise inside doubled. Lex stepped forward and jerked back the flap to reveal . . .

Eric's back was turned. The docile lizard was cradled in his arms. It appeared to be sleeping. Meanwhile Eric was kicking things, thumping the limp animal's tail against the side of the tent and making noises: "Ow! Unhhh! Let me go!"

Hearing the noise behind him, he turned and saw everyone staring at him.

A broad grin broke out on his face and he bounded out the door, the lizard snoozing in his arms.

"You jerk!" Daley said. "You nearly gave me a heart attack!"

And then the entire group dissolved into laughter.

Eric took a victory lap around the tent with the lizard, laughing uproariously, then ran off into the trees.

Eric set the lizard on the ground. It lay there motionless.

"Thanks, little buddy," he said. He patted it on its scaly flank, then yanked away the T-shirt. The lizard's eyes blinked open, its forked tongue slithered out, and then it scampered away into the woods.

Eric swaggered back to the camp.

"So," he said, smiling broadly, "everybody happy now? Have I paid off my debt to our glorious little society? Have my unconscionable acts earned your pardons?"

"Don't push it, Eric," Jackson muttered and brushed by him toward the fire pit. After a minute everybody else walked away, shaking their heads.

Finally, only Melissa was standing there. She looked at him unblinkingly.

Eric looked back at her and said, "What?"

She didn't say anything.

"Okay," he said. "Okay, okay, okay! I know

it was your idea that this be my punishment. I suppose you want me to thank you. So, thank you, Melissa. I guess you're the only one who knows about my iguanas at home."

She smiled and poked him in the chest. "You owe me, Eric McGorrill. *Big*-time."

Melissa

Eric owes me. He owes me huge. I mean, he is a total lazy jerk most of the time, and it is his fault that the lighter is broken—but he didn't do it on purpose. And any of us could have broken it at some point. We all need to be more careful, I guess. It is kind of nice having him owe me one, though. I'll just have to make it count when I call in that favor.

TWELVE

Lex was out at the building site checking his plans again. He had a bad feeling that there was something missing. Like there was something he hadn't gotten right.

He hadn't slept all night, trying to figure it all out. He was tired. He knew everybody else was tired, too, but they were all big guys, and, he figured, they ought to know how to do things. He was the idea guy. They were the practical ones. If there was a minor flaw in his plans, they'd work it out.

But still . . .

So he had gotten out of bed while it was still dark, made his way to the site where he kept his plans, and carried them down to the fire pit so he could read them over carefully and figure out what was bugging him.

The dome was the right concept. He was convinced of that, but even with the tools they did have, there was a problem: He had no good way to stick the pieces of the puzzle together. The basis of the geodesic dome was that all the rods were the same length, and they fit together in a series of interlocking triangles. But Lex had neglected to figure out a way to physically attach them to one another, and no one else had caught the omission.

Well ... it wasn't that he hadn't figured out *any* way of connecting them. Right now his plan was to lash the triangles together with ropes made from braided vines. But the more he thought about it, the less he liked the idea. When he'd made his model, he'd used tough grass from the marsh to bind the reeds together. But vines tended to split and fray if you bent them too hard. And, worse still, they weren't very rigid at all. If the whole thing flexed too much, it could collapse entirely.

Problem was, what was the alternative? Making the triangles had been easy. Simple geometry. You notched the ends at a sixty-degree angle and they all just slipped together. Fit tab A into slot B. But once you started hitching the triangles together, you ran out of easy ways to attach them.

He'd seen jungle gyms that were designed this way. But they were made of steel bars with flattened ends that attached together with steel screws.

On the island, they had no steel, no screws.

They trusted me, he thought, *and I've let them down.*

He wasn't sure what to do next. One thing was to think up a totally different shape for the shelter, but that would take even more time, and the other kids had been cutting and notching bamboo all day. Their work would be totally wasted if he changed the design.

He saw Nathan and Jackson coming toward him, chatting quietly as they walked. *Well,* Lex thought, *they won't be smiling for very long.* If he explained his problem, they'd get all bent out of shape. *Everybody's gotten their hopes up because you didn't think it through, Lexie.* Then he'd be reduced to the worst thing imaginable: little Nerd Boy—got theory, got no application. Great smarts, no practicals. Big brain, little clue.

"Hey, Lex," Nathan called softly. "What's up? You look kinda bummed out."

Lex scratched his head and considered telling them that his plan was turning into a disaster. But no, then he'd be the laughingstock of the island. There was a solution. There had to be! He just had to find it.

"It's okay," Lex said. "I'm working it out."

"Cool," Nathan said.

The two older boys walked past him, out toward the edge of the marsh where all the bamboo grew.

Lex felt the knot tighten in his stomach.

That morning they worked. And worked. And worked.

Around lunchtime Eric, Jackson, and Nathan took a break. But before lunch they sat around on the beach sharpening their hatchets and machetes, along with Jackson's knife.

Jackson was glad for the break. They had been cutting bamboo for hours—but it was time to get their tools back into working order. That bamboo was tough stuff. It dulled their blades quickly. Fortunately Lex had brought back some odd black stones from one of his forays into the jungle. They were perfect for sharpening the blades.

The girls were over by the tent, braiding vines into twine and weaving fronds into pallets and eventual wall coverings.

"So what is this stuff, anyway?" Nathan asked, holding up one of the stones Lex had found.

"Lex said it was lava rock," Jackson answered. "Pumice."

"Oh."

"Where does that kid get all this stuff?" Eric asked.

Jackson shrugged.

"*The Flintstones*, probably," Eric went on and laughed. "Maybe that makes us all cavemen. Only without Dino."

"Well, it sure makes cutting that bamboo easier," said Jackson. "I don't care where he finds the stuff."

"What a nerd," said Eric.

Jackson looked slowly over at him. "Why are you always getting on his case, Eric? You were ten once. It isn't a lot of fun to be the only little kid in a group. Right, Nathan?"

"Yeah," Nathan agreed.

"Okay, okay. I'm wrong. Again. Are we gonna have another trial and take another vote?"

"We better put all that behind us, guys," said Nathan. "And let's just hope nothing like that has to come up again."

"Yeah, right," Eric muttered.

"Hey, you're the one who put people at risk, Eric," Jackson said.

"Yep," Nathan said. "And don't forget that there were some people there who spoke for you—or who didn't vote to get you punished, anyway."

"Sure," Eric muttered.

"Well, you're sitting with one of them right now," said Nathan, nodding his head at Jackson. "Did you ever thank him?"

"No, he never did," Jackson answered quickly. "And I never expected him to, because I didn't do what I did or say what I said to get his thanks."

There was the *swish-swish, whish-whish* of the pumice on the blades as they continued their work.

"Besides, it was Melissa who saved your hide,

I'd guess," Jackson went on, looking over directly at Eric as though waiting for a reply.

Eric said nothing.

"Why did she come up with that as a punishment, Eric?"

Eric glanced up quickly at Jackson, then down again. "Who knows why Melissa does anything? We all needed that thing not to be in the tent, and everybody else was scared of it."

Jackson raised one eyebrow skeptically, then went back to sharpening his knife. It had a long, unusually shaped blade, but the handle was crudely made and wrapped with duct tape.

"You really take care of that knife, don't you," Nathan said.

Jackson shrugged. After a pause he added, "I made it myself."

"Cool!" Nathan said. "How?"

Jackson shrugged. "Kinda complicated to explain."

They waited as he scraped away at the blade.

"Well, I used the school's equipment to make the handle," he said finally.

"Man," Eric said. "If they'd caught you with that thing at school, you'd have been outta there so fast it would have made your head spin."

No kidding, Jackson thought.

"Where'd you get the blade from?" Eric said.

"Told you. I made it."

"The whole thing? Don't you need, like, equipment or something?"

Jackson nodded, then tested the blade, running it along his arm. It was so sharp now that it shaved the hair right off.

"Whoa!" Eric said. "Bet you could kill somebody with that."

Jackson felt his old street-smart instincts kicking in—an alarm bell went off in his head like the sudden clang of a fire truck you didn't even know was sitting right next to you. His defenses automatically went up.

"It's a tool, Eric," Jackson said.

"You ever stab anybody, Jackson?"

Jackson looked up and gave Eric a hard look.

"*Have* you, Jackson?" Eric was looking at him with his innocent face, just a hint of challenge in it.

There was a long silence. Jackson knew kids at the school had made jokes about him being in a gang and stuff like that. Jackson just stared at Eric.

"Don't," Jackson said finally.

Eric twitched, shrugged his discomfort, made a slight squawking attempt at a laugh, and nodded his head.

"Hey," he said. "Whatever, Jackson. I was just making conversation, is all."

"Yeah, well, don't," said Jackson.

Eric hopped up quickly. "Gosh! Look at the time! I'll bet Lex would appreciate it if he got some help cutting bamboo."

Jackson let him go and went back to sharpening.

Swish-swish, whish-whish.

As Melissa walked toward Daley, who was talking intently to Lex, she noticed that Daley looked stressed out. Not that she didn't have reason to be, of course, after the whole thing with Eric. That had been stressful for everybody. But it was a different look. *Haggard,* Melissa thought. *Weird word for describing a sixteen-year-old.*

"Hey, Daley," she called out when she saw Lex leaving. "Want me to do some more weaving? Or should I keep notching bamboo?"

"Actually, I could use help weaving some palm fronds," Daley answered. She gathered up some strips of palm frond and started weaving them together. "Here, just do it like this." She showed Melissa a pile of what looked like huge place mats woven from the green palm-tree leaves.

"So, what are we making?" Melissa said.

"They'll get laid over the bamboo framework," Daley said. "Then we'll weave more fronds into them to channel rain off the top of the structure."

Melissa concentrated on the weaving for a while. It wasn't very hard. Quickly her hands got into the rhythm of crossing over and under, over and under. Once she'd gotten the hang of it, she said, "Well, have you recovered from yesterday yet?"

"Eric, you mean? I don't know if I'll ever get

over that, Mel. That whole thing really got to me."

"Well, it had to be done, I guess."

"It's just . . . I'm getting sick of being the bad guy."

"You sound like Jackson."

Daley said nothing.

They worked quietly for a time again, then Melissa looked sideways at Daley and said, "Has Nathan talked to you lately?"

"Nathan? No."

"Oh."

"Why?"

"Hmmm, well, no reason. We've all noticed that the two of you have been around each other a lot."

"Melissa, have you noticed the size of the beach we're living on? It's hard not to be around someone a lot. I'm around Taylor a lot, too!"

"I know, I know, but Taylor doesn't follow you around all day, either."

"Well, he said something about not being in competition anymore, and I thought that was strange—nice, but strange—so I was suspicious for a while. But I guess he must have meant it."

"Oh, yeah. He *definitely* meant it."

Daley looked up at her, slightly puzzled. "What are you getting at?"

"Uh . . ." Melissa hesitated. She was on thin ice here. Nathan had been trying so hard to talk to Daley. But it kept not happening. Now Melissa thought maybe she ought to help him out a little. Or maybe that would be a huge mistake. Hard to know.

"*What*, Melissa?"

"Well . . ." Melissa hesitated, then finally took the plunge. "Daley, Nathan really likes you."

Daley rolled her eyes.

"For real, Daley! He's been going crazy trying to tell you." As soon as she said it, though, she felt like she'd totally said the wrong thing. But it was too late. She clapped her hands over her face. "Oh, great!"

"Wait a minute, wait a minute," Daley said. "You're serious?"

"Haven't you noticed how distracted he's gotten? This morning a tree nearly fell on him."

"What?"

"Yeah, Eric got all tree crazy. So he sawed down another tree—who knows why?—and Nathan was walking right where it was going to fall. Eric nearly had to tackle him to get him out of the way in time."

"Melissa, that's awful!"

"He told me he was gonna talk to you—which I encouraged him to do—then he gets scared, then he's gonna tell you again, then he backs out again." Melissa sighed. "I'm such an idiot. I shouldn't have said anything to you. *Please* don't tell Nathan I said anything."

"Well, if he wants to talk to me, why doesn't he

talk to *me* instead of you?"

"He's tried, Daley. That's what I'm trying to tell you. But something always comes up, or you have to be off saving the world or whatever." The second she said that she was sorry. "Oh. Daley, I wasn't trying to be mean. Honestly."

"Hey, no, I understand." They continued working side by side for a long time. Then Daley blew out a short breath. "Gotta go, I guess."

"Where?"

"Oh, just making the rounds. Make sure Eric's not playing, check and see if Lex is okay, get Taylor off her duff—the usual."

"Daley? You look so tired. You ought to go out walking down the beach somewhere every day— anywhere away from here. You know, just to get away for an hour every now and then."

Daley nodded her head. "Good idea, Melissa. Right. That *is* a good idea." Daley got up at that point and started off, but after just a few paces she turned back to face Melissa. "It's getting to be too much, Mel. I need to relax. You're right. I totally need to relax more."

Then she hustled off, disappearing into the undergrowth. Melissa could hear her voice, calling to people, shouting instructions and encouragement.

Melissa shook her head slightly and hoped she hadn't messed anything up for anybody. At least not too much.

THIRTEEN

"**M**elissa! How could you!" Nathan couldn't believe what she'd done. "How could you possibly have done this to me?"

"I know I shouldn't have, Nathan. I didn't mean to. And I wasn't going to. But Daley and I were working together and we got to talking, and she looked so awful, and I thought maybe you had already talked to her—I'd forgotten whether you were *going* to or *not* going to. You did change your mind a lot, and what I remembered from the last time we talked about all this was that you said you were going to. So I asked if you'd said anything. I was hoping to get her cheered up. She looked so awful."

"Oh my God, Melissa. Now it's all ruined!" Nathan started pacing up and down.

"You don't know that, Nathan. Actually, I don't think she's ever seen you as someone other than a competitor. She just never . . ."

"Thought I could like her a lot?" he finished.

"Well, yeah. I mean, neither did you, Nathan. I *am* sorry, and I know there's nothing I can really *do* now to help, but . . ." and she held out her hands in a gesture of impotence.

"So now what?" he went on, but less angry-sounding.

"You have to talk to her, Nathan."

"I've tried to—two or three times! You know that! But she's always rushing around, rushing around, rushing around. It's like she never stops. Except to sleep."

"You'll find the right moment."

Nathan felt flushed, embarrassed, nervous, sweaty, weird. Why'd Melissa have to open her big mouth? "Did she freak out, Mel?"

"She just looked at me. You know, the way she does sometimes. Looks through you more than at you?"

He actually groaned aloud.

"She's out walking around. Talk to her when she gets back, Nathan. She's had a lot on her mind."

"So have I, Melissa!"

"Yes, but not like that. You just need to watch out for falling trees."

"Oh, it might as well have hit me! She'll

probably blab it to everybody: 'My big rival has a crush on me. Isn't that hilarious?' Now everybody's gonna think I'm a joke."

"When did you change your name to Eric? You're getting to sound like him!"

Nathan sighed. He tried to think what he should do. But he was at a loss. He supposed he was just going to have to bite the bullet and talk to her. "Okay, okay, okay. I'm gonna talk to her. I am. I'm gonna talk to her."

Melissa just looked at him.

"What?" he said. "I'm gonna *talk* to her."

"Lex," Daley called to her brother. "Listen, I'm gonna take a little walk along the beach. Where's a good place to go?"

"What're you looking for?" he asked.

"Well, nothing really. I just wanted to take a little walk. You know, stop to smell the roses."

Lex frowned at her, puzzled. Daley never did stuff like that. "If you say so."

"Seriously. You've explored a lot. Where's a good place?"

"Go straight out past the marsh and keep on going."

"What's there?"

"There're some cool dunes. Really huge. The coast curves away from us to the right, so you can't see them from here. But there are two or three in a row down there. And if you go on a little farther the beach rises some, and there's a really neat cove with this sort of volcanic cliff around it. You can cross it at low tide, but it fills up at high tide, and you'd have to go into the jungle to get around it. If you want to go farther than that, there's also some really cool volcanic rock that—"

"Thanks, Lex. I just wanted to go smell the roses."

"There aren't actually any roses out there, Daley—"

"I'm aware of that."

"—but they've got turtles all over. You can see their tracks and the holes to their tunnels. And those flowers that close up at night and open the next morning?"

"Morning glories?"

"I guess."

"Okay, Lex. I'll be back in a while. Take care."

"Right."

Lex turned to keep on with whatever he had taken up to do when he thought of something.

"Daley," he called.

"Yes?"

"Be careful."

She grinned. "You know me," she said, laughing. "I never take chances."

FOURTEEN

Nathan

Melissa's right. I guess I have to talk to Daley now. We can't avoid the subject forever. At least if I catch her on her walk we'll be alone. No stupid interruptions, nowhere to hide—just me and her.

Too bad that's scarier than anything else we've encountered on this island so far.

Over by the canebrake, Nathan saw Jackson cutting bamboo. Now that Melissa had let the cat out of the bag, he really had to talk to Daley.

"Did you see Daley go past here, Jackson?"

"Yeah. A while back."

"Can you remember when?"

"No, but it's been a while. I don't remember exactly." He stopped cutting bamboo and looked up at the sky. "It's been a good while, Nathan. Couple hours? She was headed up past the marsh. Going up toward the big dunes."

"Thanks, Jackson."

"Anything wrong?"

"No. But"—he paused and looked worried—"I thought she'd be back by now, is all. She probably just lost track of the time."

"Well, there's no way for her to get lost, at least. Unless she went into the jungle, which I doubt she'd do."

"Right—and thanks, Jackson."

Nathan was able to pick up her footprints in the heavy, damp sand for a while. He followed them down to the ocean where he gathered she must have done some wading, then he caught sight of the footprints again farther on. At one point they went away from the water up to the much drier sand, and in there somewhere he lost her trail.

What was she looking for? No way she'd just go for a walk for no reason.

He increased his speed as well as he could, but that meant he had to get back down to the harder sand near the edge. Normally he would have played with the surf, moving down close, then veering away as a higher crest broke, racing up the sand toward him. But that afternoon he wasn't in much of a playing mood.

He hadn't ever been up the beach that far, but he had heard about the dunes and the cove, so he kept a lookout for the dunes. After a fairly long walk he saw them ahead, rising up slightly and a little eerily above the beach. As he got closer, he could see that there were three of them in a row from the edge of the beach on back toward the jungle. They formed a water break, a kind of natural levee—three crests formed two pretty deep gullies—and it occurred to him that a camp up there had some advantages over where they had ended up by chance in the plane crash. They were much more exposed to the waves down where they were, unless they moved farther back into the jungle. And while *that* had its advantages, it seemed to have more disadvantages, too.

Nathan climbed up to the top of the first dune, stopping to look around carefully from that height. He shielded his eyes from the sun, but saw nothing that looked like Daley. Eventually the dunes settled down into the regular shoreline, and shortly after that he could see the beginnings of some irregularity in the island. The shoreline veered off to his right pretty sharply, and the sand was strange: It was black on this beach, as though it had been burned. He supposed it was just volcanic rock. But it seemed gloomy. Even the sound from the surf was different here—harsher, somehow, and in his present state of mind, more threatening.

Still no sign of Daley.

He broke into what his great-great-grandfather—a famous explorer who had written a book about his exploits—called a "scout's pace," one that wasn't quite a jog and could be kept up for a very long time.

After a few minutes of that, he still couldn't see Daley. This was getting spooky. The surf was breaking on huge black rocks now—the waves bigger, the ocean darker.

Finally he broke into a run, heading toward what had to be the cove Lex had told him about. He was aware of a slight incline as well as rockiness underfoot. He slowed to catch his breath. Then he stopped, stooping over to gasp for real. *Running in sand is not for sissies!* he thought. It seemed to suck at his feet, making every step twice as hard as it would be on normal ground. The sand grew blacker and blacker, with occasional small jagged shards of rock in it.

When he recovered his breath and started walking again, he could soon see the cove over the crest of the fairly low rise, but the edge looked ragged. He wasn't too high above the water—no more so than on the dunes—but it seemed wilder terrain somehow, as though he had left one world and entered another.

He looked around quickly to take in the whole panorama, then began scanning the area more closely, looking for any sign of Daley. Footprints, discarded clothes, anything. He was breathing hard, and his heart was pounding. It didn't seem to be from running, though.

He didn't see anything—or anyone—down in the cove, but he quickly checked the tide and realized it was coming in. What he saw was that the curve of the land right there was such that when the tide did rise, it came in fast, whirling up eddies in the cove as well as near the shore.

Undertows, he thought. What if Daley had slid down the hill toward the cove? Or even fallen in the water! If Daley had hurt herself, she could have been swept out or even been pounded against some of the larger rocks down below.

He got out farther over the edge of the hill, looking around frantically.

Then he saw her.

She was on the other side of the cove on her back, and from where he was standing it looked like she had slipped and fallen, and was either unconscious or had a leg stuck between the rocks. Whatever it was, she was down near that incoming tide. He didn't know how high it would get, but he wasn't going to leave anything to chance.

"Daley!" he shouted.

She didn't seem to hear him.

"Daley!"

Still, she didn't move.

He scrambled down the hillside toward her, nearly falling several times. The distance across the water in feet or yards wasn't all that much, but it was clear that it didn't have to be. He knew from his own ocean-swimming adventures at home that if you didn't know the bottom of the area you were swimming in, you could get into trouble fast—really fast.

But did he have time to go clear around the cove on those rocks? Would it be quicker to take off across the water itself? He didn't know. And he didn't know the odds for one or the other.

What he *did* know was that it was crunch time, and whatever you do in crunch time, you had to commit to. Totally.

Scampering, sliding, slithering down the hillside as fast and as best as he could on the wet and treacherous rocks, he shouted at Daley over and over and over. *Hopefully she's fine. Maybe she's just resting, right? Taking a snooze in the sun?*

A small wave hit the rocks, wetting the sand not more than three feet from her face. Any second she was going to wake up and sit up and stretch and . . .

But she didn't move.

"Daley!" Maybe his voice would penetrate. Everything was probably fine, right? But maybe not. He called her name again and again.

Just in case.

FIFTEEN

Melissa looked up from her work as Jackson approached. He'd been cutting bamboo for a while, and his arms were loaded with it.

"This okay right here?" he said.

"Sure."

He dumped the clattering load of bamboo on the sand near her. Then, instead of leaving, he just stood there, looking around.

"Everything okay?" she said.

"Yeah. Only . . ." He looked around. "You seen Daley and Nathan?"

"Not for a while. I think Nathan kind of had something he wanted to talk to her about."

Jackson looked puzzled. Then it seemed to dawn on him. "Oh!" he said. "I get it."

"They probably just need a little space."

"Yeah," Jackson. "Probably."

He kept standing there.

"Are you worried?" she said finally.

"Nah," he said. "Nah, you're right. They're fine."

"Daley, Daley, Daley!" Nathan screamed as he splashed into the cove water. It wasn't that deep yet, only up to his knees—but it was coming in fast. Scary fast.

He pushed against the surge of waves, his feet digging into the sandy bottom. The water was getting deeper. Although he slipped several times, almost falling, he didn't feel it was panic time and a rational part of him knew he was okay. But he still had to get over to Daley and up to where she was on the rocks, see what kind of condition she was in, then probably get her back across the cove.

The water was nearly midthigh but he was making good progress, and he hoped there wasn't some kind of drop-off that would pull him under the surface or suck him out of the cove entirely. If *that* happened he could be in trouble, because there was no telling how far out into the ocean he could be swept. But he figured his luck was holding when the water started getting shallower and shallower. He was almost out before he realized he had lost both his shoes. That wasn't good, but he had never taken his eyes off Daley, and he clambered out of the water and up toward her on the rocks.

When he got to her, he saw she was conscious, but barely. And it was obvious she was in serious pain.

"Oh my God," he said as he looked down at her leg. She apparently had slipped and twisted it on her way down in the fall. It could be that she had gotten a foot caught in a crack. Her kneecap was on the inside of her leg, and her shin was sticking out at an odd angle.

Nathan's stomach turned as he looked at the damage. Clearly she wouldn't be able to walk away from there, and he was terrified that the pain could cause shock—if it hadn't already. Shock could make you stop breathing. He had seen that kind of injury before. One of the offensive linemen on the football team had had the same thing happen to him. Nathan had watched the coach reset his knee so at least no more damage could be done.

"Daley," he shouted. "Daley, wake up. Wake up."

She opened her eyes and looked up at him without seeming to recognize anything. "What happened?" she asked. Then she started crying, her mouth twisted by pain when she tried to move her leg.

"Don't move, Daley. I'll fix that knee for you. You just lie still and let me pop your knee back in place."

She nodded, looking at him the whole time he was getting ready to work on her leg.

"It'll probably hurt when I pop it," he said, working hard to keep his voice sounding calm. He kept talking to her while his hands did the work, hoping the sound of his voice would be enough of a distraction so she wouldn't feel the pain too much. He talked and talked, because he knew he would have to get it right the very first time or she might not let him touch her again. And he *had* to get her kneecap back in place. All the time he was cupping her kneecap in his left hand, he was gently levering her leg itself to get the feel of where things were.

Then she shrieked and relaxed.

Nathan looked down to see her leg straight again.

Yes! Her knee looked normal. Hopefully that would ease her pain a little. She needed ice. But of course . . .

"Daley," he whispered, "we'll sit here just another minute or two, but then we've got to get back across the cove."

She nodded and took a deep breath.

"Is it all right now?" she asked.

"It'll be sore for a long time. But everything's back where it ought to be. You won't be walking on it too soon, and you may have to use a stick as a crutch to help you move around, but it's going to be okay."

She nodded.

"Okay, then. We'd better get started back across the cove, 'cause we've got a long way to go."

She nodded again, and her face had regained some color.

Nathan looked at the rising tide, and it didn't seem to be as forceful anymore, so he decided that it would be a lot easier on him if he could carry Daley across the water to the other side, then figure out a way to get her over the rocks. *Well,* he thought, *we'll just have to see when we get back over there.*

"Okay, Daley, I'm going to help you get to your feet."

She nodded.

"Once you're up, see how much pressure you can put on your leg."

She nodded again.

Slowly he helped her stand, making sure there was decent footing. He didn't want her slipping on any rocks or loose dirt. He held her securely under her arms, letting her grab hold of his shirt. As she put her foot down he saw her wince. Then she let out a little gasp.

"I'll try," she whispered, teeth gritted. But her face had gone white.

"You know what?" he said. "I think it'd be best if I just carried you across the water. It'll be a shorter trip than going through the jungle around the rim of the cove."

Then for a minute he had this fantasy, like he could make a cell phone call and some team of grown-ups—medical experts with creased uniforms and shiny equipment—would come flying down in a chopper, and they'd all jump out and run over and . . . and everything would be fine.

But it wasn't like that.

There would be no rescue. Nobody would come to save them. There was no backup plan. It was all on him. *All* on him.

What if he couldn't do it? What if he wasn't up to it? A choking fear ran through him. For a moment he couldn't move.

"Nathan?" Daley said. Her voice was thin and weak. Nothing like the usual Daley, the girl who was always in charge, the girl who never showed weakness, never backed down, never lost, never cried. "Nathan!"

It snapped him out of his paralysis. *Time to move.*

"Okay," he said. "I'm gonna squat down. Just get on my back. Like a piggyback ride."

She nodded.

"Just keep your arms around my neck, and keep your legs as high as you can. There's still a lot of current here, and the less either of us gets into the water, the better. The tide's coming in, so we need to get moving before it's too deep to get across."

She nodded again.

He turned around and let her climb onto his

back. Not too bad. He eased down the rocky hill, waded into the water, and started across. At first it was no big deal. The water was slower than it had been earlier. In fact, it was kinda cool. He didn't mind the feel of her breath on his neck, her arms around his shoulders. But then as he got out toward the middle of the cove, the sand under his feet dropped off a little. The tide was coming in fast. It had slowed the current, but the water was already a lot deeper than it had been a few minutes ago.

Suddenly it was up to his chest. He staggered. The current picked up, slamming him sideways.

"You okay?" Daley said.

"I'm fine. I'm fine."

"'Cause I don't think I could swim if the current starts pulling us out into the water."

"I'm fine," he said. But he wasn't sure. The water was pushing harder and harder. Now it was up to his neck. Each time a wave came through, it threatened to lift him off his feet. He was trying to go in a straight line, but the current was pushing him out toward the sea.

"Nathan!" Daley said. "Um . . . Nathan?"

"I'm trying! I'm trying!" Nathan said.

One more wave hit him and he lost his footing. For a moment he was afraid they would be knocked over.

"Nathan!" Daley spluttered, a wave crashing over her head.

"Just hang on!" Nathan shouted. He was

swimming now, the sand under his feet so far down that he couldn't reach it. He was swimming and Daley's weight was pressing him down, and he wasn't sure he'd make it. In fact, for one terrifying moment, he realized that it was impossible.

They just plain weren't going to make it.

"You seen Nathan?" Eric said.

Taylor looked around curiously. "Matter of fact, I haven't."

Eric frowned. "Weird."

Taylor looked at him for a moment. "What— you're not *worried*, are you?"

Eric looked at his watch. "It's been, like, two hours," he said. "You know the way they are. Always grinding it in your face, how hard-working they are? It's just weird."

"You *are* worried!" she said. "You're actually *worried* about another human being!"

"Me?" Eric's eyes widened. "Hey, come on!"

Taylor stood up. "Where's Jackson?" she said. "Jackson'll know what to do."

I can't do this! It's too deep!

Nathan felt himself sinking. He thrashed

furiously at the water, feeling almost angry. If he was going down, baby, he was going down swinging.

But there was no air.

Air, air! I need air!

And then, suddenly, there was something solid under Nathan's feet. Just a whisper of sand. He dug his toes in, surged forward.

The sand was more solid now. He drove off the sand, and his head cleared the water for a moment. He sucked in air, sank again, salt stinging at his eyes.

"Nathan!" Daley yelled. Her voice sounded muffled.

The current was still pulling hard at him. But now he had solid ground under him. He pushed hard, cleared the water, took another breath, and headed for the shore.

A couple more strides and his head was safely out of the water. The current kept sucking at him and he kept pumping forward, leaning into the current.

Finally he reached the shore, gasping for breath. "Oh, man!" he said, his lungs on fire from the exertion, his thighs burning. "I gotta set you down."

Daley put her good leg down, then slowly released her grasp on his shoulders. Nathan put his hands on his knees and caught his breath. Then he looked up. The hill above them seemed endless. And it was steep, too.

"I don't think I can carry you up," he said.

"It's okay," she said. "I'll just slide up backward."

Nathan nodded, took a few more breaths. "Let's go," he said. "The tide's coming in. This whole stretch will be under water in a minute. I'll brace your foot so you don't fall."

Daley nodded her head again, and they started their slow ascent.

When they cleared the crest, Daley tried to stand up. "I don't think I can walk," she said.

"I'll have to make a carrier for you, a travois of some sort."

"A what?" Daley was looking pale again.

"It's a thing I found in my great-great-grandfather's book. The Indians used them to drag heavy stuff behind their horses."

"Heavy stuff?" Daley cocked her head. "You think I'm heavy?"

Nathan flushed. "No, I didn't mean—"

She laughed. "I'm just kidding." She moved slightly, putting more weight on the bad leg. Then she winced. "Ow! Okay! Lying down now!"

Nathan disappeared into the jungle. He returned with two large tree limbs and some vines. He set the two limbs, each about eight feet long, on the ground about three feet apart. Then he connected them with the vines in an intricate lacing. The result was essentially a stretcher.

"There we are," he said proudly to Daley.

She smiled a little, but he saw that she was really hurting.

He laid the stretcher on the sand next to her. "Roll over," he said.

She rolled onto the travois with a sharp intake of breath. Then Nathan got ready to pick up the two handles on the end of the contraption. He was going to lift up one end and drag the other, like skids on a sled.

"Hold on," she objected. "What are you planning to do? Pull me through all this sand? All the way back to the camp? It's too far, Nathan. I'm too heavy. You need to get the others."

"I'm not leaving you," he said. "Daley, you'll be light as a feather. Look, I've got another bunch of vines here. I'll string those into a sling kind of thing. They'll attach to the tops of the poles and around my shoulders. That way I won't be putting all the stress on my two arms. See? Simple. Ready?"

She nodded.

"Thank you, Nathan," she said, her voice really soft, really faint. "Thank you."

He quickly joined the twine of vines together, got them around the poles so they would stay, put himself into his harness, and started trudging back to camp.

But it was a hard slog. Nathan had known it would be—but however bad he was expecting it to be, it was even worse. He had to stop a lot more often than he had thought he would, but he also wanted to make sure Daley hadn't passed out or gone into shock. Plus, he really did want to make sure she wasn't sliding off the travois.

So he forged on, paying as little attention to where they were as he could—just keeping an eye on the tide and looking for the dunes as a mark of how far they had gone. Still, he finally let himself admit his feet were killing him. The soles of his feet had gotten pretty toughened in their two weeks on the island, but he'd never had to haul this much weight barefoot.

He rested again, checking on Daley, who seemed to be all right but still looked uncertain and scared.

"We're making it, Daley," he said at one rest. "I can see the dunes ahead. After that we're totally there."

She smiled vaguely, knowing that even once they hit the dunes, they still had a long way to go.

He rested a little. Neither of them talked. Daley just lay on the stretcher, staring at the sky.

"Nathan," Daley said at their next stop. "Why don't you leave me here right now and go back yourself to the camp and get help? I'll be fine."

He didn't say anything, just shook his head.

"Nathan, be reasonable," she said sharply. "You're exhausted."

And it was true. He was totally beat. The harness vines were cutting into his shoulders. His hands were burning. His feet were sore. But he wasn't leaving her. He just wasn't.

"We're almost there," he said. Then he picked her up and started plodding on again. For a minute he thought he might not be able to hold her anymore. Then he felt something on his hand. He looked down to see what it was.

It was Daley. She had reached behind her head and put her hand on his. Whoa! Daley putting her hand on him like it was nothing! He felt a surge of energy, and he picked up the pace a little.

And then, after another ten or fifteen minutes, he thought he heard yelling. He stopped, looked up, and saw kids running toward him. He was so focused on what he was doing, putting one foot after the other, that it took him a while to see them.

And then he realized. They were coming!

"Look!" he said to Daley, forgetting she couldn't see anything. "They're coming for us. They're practically here!"

And then the rest of the kids were pouring over the top of the big dune in front of them.

He took the harness off his neck and shouted back, waving frantically. Within a few seconds they were there. Melissa threw her arms around him. Lex hugged Daley.

"Are you okay?" everybody kept saying. "Are

you okay? What happened?"

Nathan felt a strange elation—if he could have chosen any six people in the world to be stuck on a desert island with, these were the six he would have chosen. But as everybody hugged him and slapped him on the back and told him what a great job he'd done, he felt the last scrap of energy draining slowly from his body. He hadn't realized just how much the trek had taken out of him. He must have dragged Daley close to two or three miles. And it wasn't just that. He'd been terrified, freaked out the whole time. Maybe that was the hardest part of the whole thing, how scared he was for Daley.

He flopped down on the sand next to Daley.

Then he closed his eyes, feeling the warmth of the sun spreading through his skin. *This is excellent,* he thought. *This is the happiest, fullest moment of my life.*

"We're fine," he said. "We're doing fine."

SIXTEEN

"I gotta admit, that was pretty cool," Eric said to Taylor as the group carried Nathan and Daley the last few yards back to the camp. "I'm not sure I could have carried her that far."

"Then let me remove any doubt you might have," Taylor said back. "You couldn't have."

"What's with you, Taylor? What have you got a mad-on about?"

"I don't have a mad-on about anything, Eric. I'd just like to hear you say something about how nice it was that Daley didn't get killed, or whatever. Or go into shock and have a stroke that left her a drooling idiot or something. You know?"

"Yeah, well. Sure. I guess."

Taylor looked at him without speaking.

"What!" Eric said.

"You still haven't said it."

"O-*kay*! I'm glad she didn't go into shock and come down with drooling idiot syndrome. Happy now?"

She just shook her head and walked away.

"Oh!" he called. "Because you care so much about everybody yourself!"

She kept walking, eventually reaching the tent, where everybody was still making a big fuss over Daley and Nathan.

Eric decided to go swimming. The water was perfect, the waves not too high, the temperature unbeatable. He splashed around by himself for a while, swimming on his back, doing the crawl, trying out his breaststroke. But the ocean wasn't the friendly pool back home—easier to float in, true, but too many waves to be comfortable with.

He played around, holding his hands so he could squeeze the water through his palms. But without anyone to squirt it at, that wasn't much fun.

So he just floated around looking up at the sky, relaxing in the warm water, letting his thoughts wander where they would. Just drifting, half-asleep, body relaxed, he heard a voice say, "I've never had anybody to play with."

It startled him so much, he snapped out of his

reverie and looked around. The voice had been clear and loud, and it really took him a few seconds to realize that he had been talking to himself.

I've been out here too long, he thought. *I'm losing it, dude!*

The sun went behind a cloud, and suddenly the water seemed a little cold.

He stood in the water, looking toward the shore. There was nothing special going on now. Daley was in the tent, and everybody else was messing around, making supper, carrying water, all the usual stuff.

It was like the second he was gone, they totally forgot about him. He felt a wave of self-pity. Hadn't it practically been his idea to go find Daley and Nathan? Not *precisely* his idea. But kinda-sorta. And how much credit did he get? As usual—zero.

Then he saw Melissa coming down to the water to rinse out a cook pot.

Eric started toward her. She didn't look up, didn't seem to notice he was there. He was about to wave at her, but instead he took a deep breath and dived under the surface, swimming strongly toward her. When he needed more air he surfaced slowly, barely allowing anything more than his mouth and nose to break the surface. Melissa was looking down at her pot, concentrating. He got his bearings and dived again, finally coming up behind her. She was still facing the shore when he slowly surfaced again, so he made his move.

He sprang up with a huge roar and a gigantic splash.

"Aha, me loverly!" he roared, doing his best imitation of a bad movie pirate. "I've got you now! Har har har!" And he splashed her with both hands.

She jumped and whirled around, dropping her cook pot.

"Oh, Eric, you jerk!" she shouted, then she reached into the water, feeling around blindly. "Look what you did. Now I can't find the pot."

"Well, what did you think I was, Melissa? A real pirate?"

"Yeah, right." She was fishing around in the water, looking for the pot. "God, you're like a five-year-old."

"Here, lemme help," he said.

"Just go away!" she snapped.

Eric was taken aback. Melissa wasn't usually like this. Why was she so irritated?

"What's everybody so uptight about? Taylor just snapped my head off. Now you've got your drawers in a tangle just because I was playing around. Everybody's started taking the world too seriously. Way, way too seriously. Life ought to be enjoyed more. Everybody needs to loosen up."

"No," she answered quietly. "We've all heard that way too many times from you, Eric. But I'll give you a little advice, and I hope you take it to heart. I really do."

"Oh, really? Gosh, I'm all ears."

"You've gotten to be a real bore, Eric. You're nearly seventeen years old, and here you are still acting like a child. It gets tiresome. It's boring. *You've* gotten to be boring. Grow up some."

"Thank you for the lecture. I see Daley's brainwashing campaign to turn us all into robots is working pretty great."

Melissa gave Eric a long, hard look. "Eric, you need to remember something around me."

"Like?"

"*Iguanas*, Eric. Do I need to say more? Would you like me to repeat it?"

She reached into the water again, came up with the pot, turned, and walked away.

Why's everybody walking away from me? Eric thought.

After supper that night Eric saw Lex sitting by himself drawing things in the sand with the short, sharpened stick he always carried.

"Hey, genius. Figuring out what makes clocks tick?"

Lex didn't even look up. "My name's Lex," he said, moving right along with whatever he was doing.

"So, what are you working on, *Lexie*?"

Lex was silent for a long time, and Eric seemed about to move away.

"I said my name's *Lex*."

Eric sighed and was about to leave. He stood a little longer, though, sighing some more. Then he said, "Well, I guess I'd better prepare myself for the fascinating job ahead of me tomorrow. Again."

He was a pace or two away when Lex said, "You don't like hauling water up here?"

"Oh sure, Lex. It's absolutely fun and games for me."

"You'd rather do the laundry? Chop down the trees and bamboo? Figure out things? Bring in the food—every day?"

"You got a point or just diarrhea of the mouth tonight?"

"Of course I have a point, Eric. What do you have to do for your job? I mean, what *exactly* do you do?"

Eric was silent, sizing up the boy in front of him.

"Well?"

"Okay, I'll play your dumb game. I get jugs—"

"Empties?"

"Well of course empties, dodo. Do you think I'd be hauling *full* ones down to the well?"

"See, Eric? I'm trying to help you, and you insult me. Good-bye."

"Okay. I take the empty jugs down to the well. Then I let them fill up with water. Then I haul the suckers back up here."

"And?"

"Then I pick my nose! What's with you?"

"Good-bye."

"Okay, okay. Then I empty the water into the big pot so your bigmouthed stepsister or one of the other girls can boil it."

"Then?"

"Then? Then I do it again."

"Good. What part of all that do you really, really, really hate?"

"All of it."

"Good-bye."

"The hauling, of course. What's all this about, anyway?"

"Analysis of a problem. Of course from the way you act—or *react*—most of the time, I doubt you've ever bothered trying to analyze the problem." There was a long, silent pause. "Have you?" And Lex looked up for the first time in the conversation and stared directly into Eric's eyes.

Eric looked away.

"So what have you been thinking about all this time? You could have been thinking about how to make the worst part of your job a little easier."

"Dude, it's not like we got water pipes here."

"We don't?"

Eric rolled his eyes. "Just 'cause I'm not a genius doesn't mean I'm an idiot, *Lex*."

"Good-bye."

"You really think I'm stupid, kid?" He was screaming by now.

Lex looked up at Eric one more time and made very gentle shooing motions with the back of his hands as he softly said, "Good night."

Eric turned and stalked away.

Nathan had been so worn out that he had taken a nap the second he got back to the camp. But now he was waking up. He sat up, still feeling like a truck had hit him. He stretched and went down to the fire pit to see Daley, who was still sitting there next to the cold remains of the fire Eric had ruined.

"So, how're ya doin'?" he asked, sitting down next to her.

"Good," she said. "But not ready to talk a lot. You know, about, well . . ."

Nathan was feeling a little odd now, too. Not quite sure how he felt about what had happened that afternoon. He just kept thinking about her hand touching his as he pulled her.

"Hey, don't worry," he said. "I don't have anything to say, either."

"No, it's not that." She hesitated. Their eyes met for a second, then she looked away. "What you did this afternoon—it told me all I need to know about you. It's just that there are still things I have to say, but now isn't the time. Do you understand?"

"Sure, sure," Nathan nodded. But he didn't

really know exactly what she was talking about. "Well, guess I'd better turn in. You need help getting back to the tent?"

"No, Lex and Jackson rigged up a crutch for me. Wasn't that nice of them?"

He smiled weakly and nodded. He wanted to be different from them. Didn't want to just be somebody else doing something nice. Anybody could be nice. He wanted more than that.

But the way she'd held his hand when he was dragging her across the sand . . . didn't that mean something? He wanted to ask her about it. But at the same time he didn't.

"What?" Daley said.

"Nothing. Guess I'll go."

"Oh," she said as he turned to go, "I'd like to have a council meeting tomorrow. I've been thinking things over, and I really need to talk to everybody."

"About?

"Things. How we do some things. Not really a big deal—I hope!"

"Sure. Yeah. Okay." Right now he didn't really care about council meetings.

He paused for just another second, then looked at her. She reached up to him, and their hands touched.

"See ya."

"Yeah."

He headed back into the darkness toward the tent.

SEVENTEEN

The next morning after their cold breakfast, Daley gathered everybody around the fire pit. Even though there was no longer a fire, they had gotten used to assembling there.

"We've still got a lot of work to do on the shelter, guys, so I'll get started right away. But first, I want to thank you all from the bottom of my heart. Nathan especially, for obvious reasons, but all the rest of you for helping out the way you did."

Everybody nodded. Melissa patted Nathan on the shoulder.

"But anyway, what I want is for us to talk about changing the way we do some things around here."

People stirred a little at that.

"Here's what I'm proposing. Up to now we've

voted to elect one person as a kind of leader.
Jackson was first, then me. I haven't wanted to
call it 'leader' so much as 'organizer' or 'referee'
or something. But whatever you call it, being the
leader means that you're the bad guy all the time.
The reason I fell down that hill yesterday was that I
was getting sick of the pressure. So I wandered off
somewhere I probably shouldn't have, just to get
away from it for a while."

Jackson nodded. Daley knew he understood
how she felt because he'd been there.

"Back in the day," she said, "the ancient Romans
used to choose their leaders on a revolving basis.
You'd be consul—that's what they called them—for
a year, and then somebody else would take over
for a while. What if we did the same thing?"

They all looked around at one another. But
nobody spoke.

"That way everybody has to share the
responsibility of the job, so it doesn't always fall on
the same person forever. I also think that it would
help *all* of us to see our world from that point of
view. You know, so it isn't the same person playing
the bad guy every single time when it comes to
decisions and organizing and getting work done.

"So, if you want to talk about it now, I'm good
with that—I can't walk away real fast anyhow. But
if you want to think about it some more, then I'm
good with that, too. But I think it's time we thought
about that kind of thing." She looked around the
ring. "Uh . . . that's it."

They all sat around for a few minutes—some twitching, some staring at the jungle, some looking around at the others.

"It might be a good idea," Melissa said, "if we thought about it for a while. Then later this afternoon we can talk about it more."

There was a general murmur of consent.

"How's five o'clock sound?"

"I need to check my calendar," Nathan said. "I might have something scheduled."

Everybody laughed.

Within minutes, everyone was hard at work. The sounds of tools echoed across the beach.

They worked until lunch, then ate more cold food. No more cooking, now that Eric had trashed their fire. Not that anybody really noticed.

After lunch Melissa looked around and smiled. Building the shelter had given them a sense of purpose that they hadn't had in a while. Dozens of triangular pieces—the building blocks of Lex's dome design—were stacked up on the sand. Neatly piled ropes of braided vine lay next to them. It was hard to believe that they'd made so much progress. It was amazing how much they could accomplish when everybody was cooperating. She felt a surge of pride.

The dog tags of the World War II soldier still hung on the pole where Jackson had put them, sparkling in the sunlight. If the group just stuck together, surely they wouldn't end up that way, lost for another half century until somebody found a few puzzling and incomplete remains to indicate their existence here.

In an uncharacteristic move, Taylor sidled up next to Melissa.

"Hey," Taylor said. "Um, I'm heading over to the wing. There're some good vines over in the trees behind it. Wanna join me?"

Melissa looked at her for a second, surprised. In the two weeks they'd been here, it was the first time Taylor had ever sought her out for a conversation.

"Sure," Melissa said.

They walked silently down the beach toward where the torn-off wing of the aircraft lay half-embedded in the sand.

Taylor pointed into the woods. "See."

Melissa nodded. The vines here looked exactly like the ones that were closer to the camp. "So, Taylor," she said. "There's something you wanted to talk about?"

"Melissa, what do you think about Daley's new thing? Everybody seems to be copping out on the leadership business."

"Oh, I don't know, Taylor. I don't see it as a cop-out. Not really. Why? Are you against it?"

"I don't know. I was at first, but she made it sound like it was okay. I mean, like, I got scared, I guess you could say."

"How come?"

"I don't know. There was just something spooky about it—for me, I mean. Not for Daley or Nathan or you, maybe, but for me. Melissa, we've been around each other a pretty long time, and you know me. I mean, I've never been into this kind of stuff. You know? Class president, all that crap? Boring!" She paused, a hesitant expression on her face.

Melissa waited for Taylor to make her point. Instead, Taylor walked toward the trees and started pulling down vines. Melissa followed suit.

After she'd gotten a few more vines out of the trees, Taylor finally said, "But . . ."

"But *what*?" Melissa asked.

"Yeah, well, all morning I was braiding vines, braiding vines, braiding vines. It was like my hands were working, but my brain was thinking about something else. I kept thinking . . . I mean, this is so *surreal*. You know? I mean, who'd have ever thought we'd be *here*? Like *this*? Who'd have ever thought we'd have to be even thinking about all these kinds of things? Forming a government? Making up laws? Punishing people for, like, infarctions?"

"I think that's in*frac*tions."

Taylor waved her hand. "Whatever. My point is, I mean, that's what adults do, right? That's for senators and judges and . . . people like that. Sixteen-year-old kids don't do stuff like that. And *I* sure don't. Please!"

"Okay . . ."

Taylor pulled down a vine and started wrapping it around her arm. "But . . . I got excited about it. I mean, I think I want to be the leader."

Then she turned away. Melissa wasn't sure—but it looked as if Taylor actually blushed. Taylor, who was never embarrassed about anything!

Taylor yanked on a vine for a while, but it wouldn't come down. After a minute, she moved on to another one without comment. Melissa reflected that two weeks ago, if Taylor had run into an obstacle—even a small one like this—she'd have pouted and complained and pitched a fit. And then she'd probably have quit working.

"I mean, I didn't exactly *want* to be the leader, but it just hit me, like—whoa!—maybe I could do that!" She blinked. "So what's happened to me? What's *wrong* with me?"

Melissa's first reaction was to laugh.

"What!" Taylor's eyes got hard.

Melissa tried to stop laughing. "I'm not laughing at you, I promise."

"Then what's so funny?"

"It's just . . . who'd have thought it? You know?"

Taylor's face relaxed.

"Honestly?" Melissa said. "Everybody will be glad. Daley's about had it with responsibility. Jackson doesn't want to do it. Eric's not ready. Nathan's . . . uh . . . distracted right now. So why not? I think you'd be a very good leader. You're direct. You know how to get people's attention. You've always been a leader. Just not in this way. I think it's just that you've never had any reason to do this kind of thing before. I think it'll be cool, actually."

"Really?" Taylor cocked her head.

"Really. You'll be a breath of fresh air."

"Huh," Taylor said. Then she looked up at the trees. "Do you think you can help me here? I think this one'll come down if we pull together."

"Yeah," Melissa said. "I think you're right.

By midafternoon they'd gathered enough bamboo and made enough triangles to start building the dome.

Lex called to Nathan and Jackson, who were still cutting bamboo. "I think that's enough, guys."

Nathan immediately dropped his machete and grinned. "So what's next?" he said.

"We need to get the site finished so we can start erecting the dome itself," Lex said.

"How's that gonna work?" Jackson asked.

"Follow me," Lex said.

They walked back to the site, where Lex took a moment to survey the scene.

"Where's Eric?" he said.

Nathan and Jackson looked at each other and shrugged. "He keeps going off into the jungle and disappearing," Nathan said. "I think he's just sleeping."

Lex nodded. Figured.

"This part's gonna take a lot of muscle," Lex said. "The more people we've got on it the better."

"Muscle?" Nathan said. "That rules Eric out."

"You're totally funny, dude," a voice said. They looked around and Eric was standing at the edge of the site, looking at them.

"Where you been?" Jackson said.

"I'm handling the water situation," he said, grabbing an empty jug.

"Yeah," Nathan said. "Like hauling water takes all day."

"Whatever," Eric said, disappearing back into the woods with the empty water jug.

"See?" Nathan said. "He helped us chop bamboo for about an hour this morning. Then he grabbed a load to bring back here. After that? *Finito*. Never saw him again."

"He never brought any bamboo back to the site," Lex said.

Nathan shook his head. "Figures. Probably dumped it in the woods."

"Anyway," Jackson said. "What's next?"

"Before we can put up the dome, we need to make a platform. We'll hold it up with pylons.

Then we'll make a structure of bamboo to hold up the floor. Those really big pieces of bamboo that you got from over by the marsh? That's what they're for."

Lex then explained the details to Nathan and Jackson, how the bamboo poles should be tied and wrapped together to be laid on the finished stand, and how it would all fit together.

"The stand itself is going to sit on eight pylons around the outside of the dome, with about nine pylons in the center." He pointed to marks he had made in the ground. "The pylons will be made of the biggest bamboo poles. We'll sharpen them and drive them into the sand. They'll need to go pretty deep. Maybe three, four feet. That way the shelter won't blow away in a big storm."

"But, Lex," Jackson said, "how're we gonna pound in those pylons? We don't have a hammer."

Lex gnawed on his lower lip. "Um. That's why I was thinking you might need Eric. It's just gonna be a lot of hard pounding. You'll probably want to rotate the job a little."

"We need a sledgehammer or something," Nathan added, "and those pylons would have to be at least six feet long so the thing would be solidly rooted. Then we could leave about two feet to lay the floor on, but—"

"Ohhh-kay," Lex said. "Right," he went on, hoping something sensible would occur to him.

"No hammers. No mallets. No hydraulic pile drivers."

Lex looked around for something that would work. He noticed a large chunk of wood with a crudely fashioned handle lying at the edge of the site. It wasn't exactly a sledgehammer. Sort of a mallet. But it would work.

"What about this?" he said.

"Cool!" Nathan came over, took it from Lex, and hefted it in his hand. "Did you make this, Jackson?"

Jackson shook his head.

"Huh," Nathan said, looking at it curiously. Then he shrugged. "Well, anyway, it'll work."

He picked up a big piece of bamboo and started pounding it into the ground.

Late in the afternoon they gathered around the fire pit. Everybody complained good-naturedly about their hands, their backs, their sunburns, their scratches and bruises. But there was a general sense that things were coming along well.

"Okay," Daley started, "we've had all day to think about what I suggested this morning. I'm open to suggestions, conversation, or just about anything as long as we all understand two things. First, I will be 'retiring,' or whatever you want to call it, as soon as I can. Second, we need to settle this as soon as possible. Okay? Shoot."

After a little bit of shuffling around, Taylor raised her hand. Very tentatively.

"What if someone volunteered to be leader?"

"Well, then I guess that would be that, and we could all get back to work."

"Trouble is, though," Nathan put in, "that might settle things until that person got tired or 'retired' or whatever. But if we're supposed to be working on a change in the way we've set ourselves up already, then that wouldn't settle anything over the long haul. Eventually we'd just have to go through this all over again."

"Well, do we really need to change the system we've got?" Lex asked.

Jackson and Daley answered at the same time. "Yes!"

"Aren't we supposed to vote on stuff?" Eric asked. "I mean, aren't we supposed to vote on whether we're going to change or not? Seems to me that if this is supposed to be a democracy, then we have to decide that before we decide what we'll change to."

"Absolutely," Daley granted him.

"So then, would you be willing to recap some reasons for making a change?" Nathan prodded.

Daley went through her reasons from that morning.

"Aren't those more like reasons why you

resigned than reasons for changing the system?" Eric asked.

"Not at all," Daley answered. "In this case they're the same thing. People get sick of the responsibility."

Taylor asked, "So how would it work?"

"There'd be a rotation schedule."

"How would the rotation start?" Taylor said.

Daley shrugged. "Alphabetically by last name?"

"How long a term?" Lex said.

There was silence for a good while after he asked that question. Melissa and Taylor looked over at each other for just a second and nodded. The others looked down at their sneakers or at the sand or anywhere else but at one another.

Finally Daley said, "Well, I guess we just can't answer that question, Lex."

"Then why do we need a leader at all?" Lex asked. "We can't know how long we'll be here, as Jackson said. So there's no way to know how long someone should serve as leader, and it can't ever be fair."

"So you suggest . . . what?" Nathan asked.

"I dunno. I'm just saying we've only suggested one way to regovern ourselves, and that's by electing a leader of some sort, and he or she will serve whatever term or for however long we determine. But we've already seen two guys get voted in and they've both resigned. That's two in, what, about two weeks?"

They all stared over at Lex, who squirmed under their joint gaze, but only just a little.

"So?" said Taylor.

"You've got a better solution?" said Eric.

"I've got another one. Better? Who knows?"

"And that is?" said Daley.

Lex sighed deeply.

"Consensus," he said.

No one said anything for a long time.

"What's that?" Taylor finally asked.

"Well, you sit around and talk about the things that have to be decided, and you do that until everybody's comfortable with what seems to be the plan."

Silence.

"The plan just sort of . . . emerges," Lex said. "Everybody wins, nobody loses."

"How does nobody lose?" asked Jackson.

"Well, everybody gets their say; everybody gets a chance to be heard; everybody gets something they want; everybody gets something they don't want; so nobody actually *loses* anything. That way the group decides as a group."

"No *us* versus *them*," Jackson said.

"Right," Lex answered. "It's all *we*."

"Well, if there's no voting, I'm all for it," Eric put in. "I vote against voting." And with that he held up his hand.

"Lex, does that really work?" Daley asked. She was thinking back to the time and energy put into the polling and posters and handshaking and all the rest of her race against Nathan for senior-class president, an activity now so remote, she almost couldn't imagine it, much less understand how it had consumed her—and Nathan—for so long.

Jackson stepped in before Lex could answer. "Lex, do you remember when you told me about ants and how awesomely they're organized— even though they don't have any leaders?"

"Uh-huh."

"Then you were going to tell me something about fireflies, but I sorta cut you off."

"Yeah. This is kinda cool. I read about these fireflies that live out here in the South Pacific. At home fireflies flash their lights in a random way. They all do their own thing. But here there's a species that lights up all at the same time. And nobody seems to know why. They all light up, then they all go out. Light up. Go out. All at once. So when zillions of fireflies light up their taillights at the same time, they say you can nearly read a book by the light. It lights up the whole jungle.

"So I guess the fireflies are all alike that way. And the ants. They don't seem to have a leader— at least the ants and the fireflies—but they act as a unit. Nobody knows how it works, but the consensus idea seems sort of like the same thing to me."

There was absolute silence after Lex finished, but he couldn't tell if it was from agreement or lack of attention to what he was saying.

Eric folded his arms. "So what you're saying is we should try to act like bugs," he said.

Lex glanced around the ring, looking for help.

"We're only seven kids," Jackson said. "Maybe we *can* run on a consensus mode for a while. At least we wouldn't have to worry about votes and all that. Or when somebody's term was up."

"Or if the leader got fed up and wanted out."

"Or whether there should be any rules about things."

"Or whether there should be any jungle jails."

Soon they were all talking over one another.

"Whoa!" Daley held up her hands and shouted. "Hold on a minute. This is starting to sound a lot like anarchy, guys. Even for consensus to work, there have to be some rules."

Everybody nodded.

"Then we're just right back where we started from, Daley," Eric shouted. "Rules and punishments. Votes and jungle jails. Might as well leave it as it is. People are going to do what they want no matter what."

Daley sighed and rubbed her sore leg.

Melissa stood. "It's all a matter of respect, guys. If you don't respect other people, nothing will work. If you do, anything will."

"Let's just vote," Jackson said, his voice

suddenly tired and sour. "Let's just vote on what Daley's suggested."

"I've forgotten what that was," Lex said.

"We go in turns being leader." Nathan was speaking. "When the leader gets fed up or when we get fed up with the leader, the next person on the list—alphabetically by last name—gets to be leader. And we do this until we get rescued. Who's in favor?"

Slowly every hand went up. Except for Eric's.

He looked around the group. "What?" Then slowly he raised his hands. "Okay, you want me to be a happy little firefly, fine!"

"I think fireflies would be more the consensus thing," Lex said.

"Whatever. I voted. I'm sure you're all deliriously happy." Eric stood. "Okay, see you later."

"Wait, wait, wait," Daley said. "We've got to choose the next leader. Any volunteers?"

There was a long silence. Then finally Taylor cleared her throat.

Daley turned and looked at her. "You have a suggestion, Taylor?"

"I'll start it off," she said tentatively. "I'll go first."

Daley and Jackson's eyes met. Jackson shrugged imperceptibly.

"All in favor?" Daley said.

All hands went up.

"Congratulations," Daley said.

Taylor looked around the group and smiled. "Do I get a crown or something?"

"Don't push it," Nathan said.

Everybody laughed.

"Can I go now?" Eric said. "Are we done?"

"What, you have someplace important to be?" Nathan said.

But Eric was gone.

Jackson

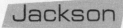

I think it will be cool for Taylor to be leader. Everyone gives her a lot of grief for being flaky, but she's not stupid—not really. When she actually cares, she can be downright clever. And no one can say she doesn't have guts. She's not afraid to say what she wants or voice her opinion. I don't think she'll make a bad leader at all... Taylor's cool.

EIGHTEEN

Lex felt pretty bummed the next morning. For the third night in a row he had barely slept. He felt that he was right back where he had been before: People never really listened to him because they just weren't interested in listening to anything they hadn't heard about before. And they didn't want to listen to him because he was just a kid.

As if they aren't kids themselves! And they didn't want to listen to him, why . . . because he compared them to ants and fireflies? As usual, Eric was the one giving him the hardest time. As if Eric ever had a single useful idea the whole time he was here.

Lex headed away from the beach and started toward the jungle to check on his garden. At least that was something they understood. Even if they didn't get why ants and fireflies were creatures to be admired, at least they knew they had to eat something besides fish and coconuts every day. And it was *Lex* who was making that possible. It was *Lex* who could find things like pumice to sharpen their stupid knives and hatchets. It was *Lex* who knew how to put a shelter up . . .

At that, he felt a sudden horrible twisting in his stomach. The shelter. They were getting closer and closer to putting all the triangles together . . . and he was further and further from a solution on how to attach them. Something about the way the triangles hooked together. They *fit* fine, but he had tested the strength and flexibility of the vines—and he just wasn't sure.

What if they just don't work? The thought almost made him sick to his stomach.

He took his time at the garden. He weeded, he transplanted, and he suckered the tomato plants that were growing like wildfire. He checked to see if insects or other predators had made inroads into the growing crop. He also checked to see if there were any signs of animals or birds dipping into his garden. He was surprised that birds hadn't already picked it bare, but it also occurred to him that they might be waiting until things had gotten just about ripe, and *then* they'd make their move.

Well, he thought to himself, *I can put up some stakes with fluttery rags on them. And maybe I can scrounge up something shiny that'll scare them away.*

So . . .

So he had to go back to the building site after all. Go back and face the music. Go back and tell them he was brain-dead. Go back and tell them . . .

. . . all their work had been for nothing.

"Where's Eric?" Taylor looked around, clearly irritated. She'd been working her fingers to the bone today—trying to set a good example, if you could believe that!—and she was a little peeved that Eric was making himself scarce, as usual.

"Where *is* Eric?" Daley said, hands on hips.

"Same old story," Nathan said. "Soon as breakfast is over, he boogies off into the woods, doesn't come back again until he smells food."

"So what's the plan, Lex?" Taylor said.

"Uh . . ." Lex looked strangely nervous.

There was a long silence.

"Well?" Taylor said. "Give it up, Lex."

Lex cleared his throat. "Well, uh . . . we just take the triangles . . . uh . . . and start lashing them together with the vines."

"You heard him!" Taylor said. She clapped her hands. "Chop-chop, everybody! I don't want to spend another night in that gross tent!"

Everybody began working enthusiastically. Taylor looked around at the group. Other than the fact that Eric was off sleeping, everything was going great. She felt a sudden burst of pride and enthusiasm. She was leading. She was totally *leading*!

What was up with Daley and Jackson? They both acted as if being a leader was such a drag. She didn't see the problem. This was easy! This was fun!

By late morning, the dome had begun to rise. First they had laid down the floor. Once that was complete, they had lashed together one course of triangles, then a second on top of that, propping up the structure with bamboo poles.

Halfway there!

Lex was feeling a little better now. The vines weren't as strong as he would have liked—but Melissa had come up with a way of wrapping them that kept them from splitting. Once the dome was erected, the poles would be pulled out and the structure would hold up on its own.

Hopefully.

"Whew!" Nathan said. "I'm getting thirsty!"

"Me too!" Melissa said.

"Let's take a break," Taylor called out.

Everybody had made cups out of pieces of bamboo. They all picked up their cups and lined up in front of the water jug. Jackson picked it up, lifted it over his bamboo cup, and turned it upside down. A glistening drop hung at the edge of the jug and fell with a tiny plop into the bottom of Jackson's empty cup.

Everyone groaned.

"Where's Eric?" Daley said.

"Eriiic!" Taylor's voice was harsh.

"Eric! Eric!" Everybody was calling now.

Eric staggered out of the jungle, two fresh new jugs of water in his hands. He thumped them down on the sand in front of Jackson.

The entire group glared at him.

He looked around innocently. "What?"

Everyone in the group shook their heads and turned away. But not so fast that Lex didn't see a superior little smirk lick at the corner of Eric's mouth. As though he was scamming everybody, carrying one load of water while all the others had knocked themselves out working all morning.

Lex felt like throwing something at him. But before he had a chance, Eric was gone.

Once things got rolling, there wasn't really much else for Lex to do. He'd engineered the plan, the older kids had agreed, and everything seemed to be going okay. Nathan and Jackson had turned themselves into project engineers and were pointing and giving instructions; Taylor was encouraging people; Daley was organizing;

and Melissa was working doggedly at whatever anybody suggested that she do.

It was a well-oiled machine.

By noon they had the fifth course of triangles up. All that was left was a hexagon made from the last set of six triangles. Once they lashed that in, they could take away the support poles and see if the dome held up. The final hexagon would be like the keystone of an arch: Once in place, the structure should be able to hold up its own weight.

Lex sidled over and shook the structure again.

"Hey!" Daley called to him. "Don't be messing with it till the final set of triangles is in."

Lex sighed. He still felt as though there was something missing here. It just wasn't rigid enough with only vines to hold it together. "Look, I really think—"

Taylor interrupted. "Everybody ready for lunch?"

"I'm starving!" Nathan said.

"I'm thirsty," Melissa said.

"I'm parched!" Daley said.

Then they all stopped and looked up at the nearly completed dome.

"But you know what . . ." Jackson said.

They all looked at one another as though they were all thinking the same thing.

"Who's for finishing it and *then* eating lunch?" Taylor called.

All hands went up.

"Okay, then," Taylor called. "Chop-chop, people! Let's do it!"

There was a flurry of work, and then the final set of triangles went up. They lifted it carefully above the half-completed dome, then Nathan and Jackson lashed the final lengths of vine onto the structure.

"Done!" Nathan called, pumping his fist in the air.

A ragged cheer went up. Lex felt a nervous excitement in his gut.

"Let's get the support poles down," Jackson said. "The structure has to hold its own weight or it won't last."

Everybody went inside the dome and started pulling out support poles. Finally there was only one left, an extra-large bamboo pole in the very center. Jackson was about to grab it.

"It's my design," Lex said. "Let me do it."

Shrugging, Jackson took his hand away from the bamboo strut.

Lex came over, took a deep breath, and yanked the bamboo pole away. Nothing moved.

The structure had held!

Everybody began cheering and slapping Lex on the back.

"You're a genius!" Taylor said.

"Let's eat!" somebody else said.

They lifted Lex up and carried him on their shoulders to the fire ring.

"Pour this man a drink!" Nathan shouted.

Melissa picked up one of the jugs. Then she turned and looked at everybody. "You're not gonna believe this . . ."

The jug was empty again. They'd been working so hard in the heat that they'd burned through all their water.

"Where's Eric?" everybody shouted. "Eric! *Eric!* Eric, you jerk!"

And suddenly Eric was standing right in front of them. "You rang?" he said.

Taylor came out and stood in front of him, hands on her hips. "This is totally, totally unacceptable!" she shouted. "Everybody here has been killing themselves. And what have you been doing? Nothing! You had one little dinky job and you couldn't even do that."

Eric cocked his head, looked at Taylor, then at Daley. "Have you and Daley switched brains or something? 'Cause I'm getting a real scary vibe here."

"Where's our water?" Daley said.

"Yeah, where's our water?" Taylor and Daley both had their hands on their hips, glaring at him.

Eric smirked. "Follow me," he said. Then he walked back into the jungle. Everybody looked at one another. Then Taylor shrugged.

They all stalked angrily after him.

They didn't have to go far, though. Eric pushed back the leaves of a rubber tree and pointed at something on the ground.

"What's that?" Melissa said.

It was a piece of bamboo. Connected to another piece. Connected to another piece. Each piece was about a foot off the ground, held up by two other pieces of bamboo, each driven into the ground. The whole contraption snaked off into the jungle, disappearing in the underbrush a hundred feet or so away.

Eric held out his hand. "Jug, please, Miss Wu," he said.

Melissa was still carrying the empty water jug. Eric put the jug under the end of the last piece of bamboo. It appeared to be plugged with a piece of wood. He pulled out the plug, and a stream of water ran into the jug.

Everyone's eyes widened as the jug slowly filled. Eventually the stream of water slowed. Just as the jug filled up, the water stopped.

"Whoa!" Lex said.

"Bamboo pipe," Eric said proudly, waving his hand at the contraption. "Seams are caulked with a natural rubber gum, thanks to our surplus of rubber trees. Leaks a tiny bit . . . but not too bad. I'll run the last fifty feet and it'll come right out next to the shelter. There's a trough at the other end, next to the well. All you have to do is scoop the water out of the well, dump it in the trough and—voilà!— it runs downhill all the way to the shelter."

"Nice," Nathan said.

"This, my friends," Eric said, handing the jug back to Melissa, "is the last jug of water yours truly will ever carry."

He walked back toward the dome, grinning from ear to ear.

Lex examined the pipe. He was amazed. It was beautiful. Using the sap from the rubber tree was a stroke of genius. He wondered what would keep the bamboo sections from coming apart, though.

They walked back to the dome.

Lex scurried after Eric. "Cool pipe," he said.

Eric just smiled.

"I'm just curious, though, how do you hold the sections together?"

Eric shrugged. "I just notched them, drilled a little hole with a drill bit I made from a bolt from the wing of the plane. Then I ran a bamboo pin through the holes, gummed it shut with rubber."

They emerged into the clearing.

"By the way," Eric said, stopping. "Nice shelter."

"Oh no!" Taylor screamed. "Oh no!"

Everybody stared. Where the dome had been before was a sagging collection of bamboo triangles. The entire structure had collapsed!

"All our work!" Daley said.

"No!" Nathan said.

And then they all lapsed into glum silence. They could hear the dull thud of waves in the distance.

Lex felt sick. He had known it was going to happen. He'd *known* it. And yet he'd been too chicken to admit he didn't have all the answers.

Everybody's eyes eventually turned toward Lex. The kids stared at him mutely, their eyes communicating anger and resentment. With food short and their strength ebbing, he had wasted two days of their lives.

For a minute Lex thought he would cry. His big plan, totally shot down. Why had he thought something this complex would ever work? They just didn't have the right materials, the right tools, the right—

"It's okay, Lex," Jackson said, patting him on the shoulder. "You tried."

But even Jackson's voice had something dismissive and condescending about it.

Then something hit him.

"Wait a minute!" Lex shouted. "Eric's got it figured out!"

"Huh?" Eric said.

"Bamboo pins!"

NINETEEN

It took Lex most of lunch to convince the discouraged group that his basic plan was still a sound one.

"All we needed were decent fasteners," he said. "And Eric found the solution."

"Come on, Lex," Nathan said, "it's a great concept, but we just haven't got all the stuff we need."

"No, hold on," Lex said. "That's what I'm saying. When I planned this whole thing originally, I kept thinking about the way a jungle gym works. It has steel bolts that hold the corners of the triangles together. And I kept thinking, well, we don't have bolts—so we pretty much have to give up on doing it that way."

"Exactly my point," Nathan said.

"Yeah, but Eric's got the solution. Bamboo

pins. Bamboo is incredibly tough. We just need to notch the ends of the triangles and then run bamboo pins through them. It'll be totally rigid then."

"Show us," Jackson said.

Lex took Jackson's knife, cut the vines lashing a couple of triangles together, and hacked away at the ends of the pieces of bamboo for a while.

"You don't happen to have any extra pins made, do you, Eric?" he said.

"Matter of fact . . ." Eric reached in his pocket and pulled out a small sliver of bamboo that had been carved into a long circular pin.

Lex pushed it through the hole he'd made, attached it to a second triangle, then shook it savagely. "Check it out," he said. "Solid as a rock."

Everybody looked at Taylor.

"What?" she said. Then, remembering her new role, she said, "Oh. Who wants to try Lex's new method? Show of hands?"

When they built the dome the second time, their practice on the first version paid off.

This time they built it on the ground and then lifted it onto the platform. It made construction easier because the support poles were short. And besides, everyone agreed, if the dome could be moved once it was built, it would definitely be strong enough to hold up next time there was a storm.

After working all afternoon—notching bamboo, drilling holes, cutting pins, and then assembling the triangles again—the dome was finished. Even Eric helped. All they needed to do was to move it up onto the platform.

"It's getting dark," Taylor said. "We still have to put all the leaves and mats on top and stuff. Should we just call it a day?"

For a moment no one said anything. The sun had just gone down, and the sky over the water was a deep orange, fading rapidly into reds and purples.

It was Eric who finally broke the silence. "Gotta be honest. I'd kinda like to see it up on the platform before we quit."

Taylor didn't ask for a vote. She just nodded.

Wordlessly, they gathered around the dome. Without anyone even directing them, they all stooped over, lifted the dome up slowly until they were all upright, then baby-stepped their way across the floor. Twice they had to set it down to rest. Then a third time. After that, they finished their walk. Lex gave the order to slowly, slowly, slowly lower the dome.

It was getting hard to see now.

"Watch your fingers," Daley called out. "They'll get crushed if you're not careful."

They lowered the dome the last few inches. It came down and fit almost perfectly. Lex had tried to make sure the flooring was slightly smaller than the circumference of the dome's base, but without a real measuring stick, there was bound to be a snag. It was a small one. At one spot the base got hung up on a piece of the flooring bamboo. They all looked at one another.

"Will it ride over?" Nathan asked.

"We'd have to rock it to do that," Jackson answered, peering closely at it.

"Will it be able to take the strain?" Melissa asked.

"If it's supposed to be strong enough to stand up to a storm, it better be able to," Eric put in. "I don't want this thing blowing off into the jungle with me in it!"

"Let's just do it," Taylor said.

Everyone nodded, then grabbed the bottom edge of the dome.

"Start rocking it gently toward me," said Nathan. He and Jackson and Lex stood close together at the spot they needed to get over. The others started pushing as the three boys lifted.

Once. Then again. Then, "One more time," said Lex.

The dome moved, slipped over the bamboo stub, and settled firmly into its trench.

For a minute nothing happened. The seven dusted off their hands and caught their breath. They still had a lot to do—putting the skin of woven palm-leaf mats onto the dome and covering that with bamboo leaves. Probably a couple of days' work. But the hardest part was done.

Then there was a moment of quiet.

Then Lex said, "We *did* it. We really *did* it."

And with that they all took up the cry: "We did it! We did it! We did it! We did it!"

Then they were hugging and crying and shouting and laughing, glancing occasionally at the dark structure to make sure it was really as solid as it seemed.

Then Jackson was standing by the entrance to the shelter, holding up an object in one hand. In the growing darkness, it was hard to make out at first. Everyone gathered around him. When he looped the thin chain around the entryway, they heard the clink of metal and saw a gleam in the darkness.

The cheers and laughter faded.

It was the dog tags of Walters, Matthew D.

"This is not us," he said softly. "We're all going home. *All* of us."

They stood silently for a moment in the gathering darkness. And then, strangely, it seemed as if the night was growing lighter instead of darker.

Everyone stopped, noticing that the faces around them had begun to glow. Not from sunlight, but from something paler and softer.

Then Lex pointed. They all turned.

In the distance something was moving and

writhing in the darkness. A dull glowing mass like a giant ghost or some kind of weird UFO. It was winking on, winking off, winking on, winking off. It grew brighter and brighter, growing, rising slowly into the air in the distant trees. It was eerie and beautiful at the same time.

"What *is* it?" Melissa whispered.

The light came on again, brightening everyone's faces with a soft, pale light.

Then Lex spoke, softly, almost to himself:

"Fireflies," he whispered. "Look at the fireflies."